B

As an undergr[a]... Jonathan King ... national hit 'Everyone's Gone to the Moon', went on to get his MA in Eng. Lit. at Cambridge, and came down to host his own national TV talk show on ITV whilst continuing to write and produce hit records. He discovered/named and/or produced Genesis, 10cc, The Bay City Rollers and The Rocky Horror Show, was in the charts many times in various disguises, twice ran Decca/London records and started his own label—UK. He also stood for Parliament twice as an independent (for fun), went to America to cover the 1980 Presidential election for the BBC, stayed on to do a daily TV show, and finally fulfilled his life-long ambition—to write a novel. Commuting now between London and New York, he considers himself a 'truly bi-continental communicator'.

To my mother—Mrs Ailsa King—
who's been waiting a long time for this!

BIBLE TWO

**A novel according to
Jonathan King**

A STAR BOOK

published by
the Paperback Division of
W. H. ALLEN & Co. Ltd

A Star Book
Published in 1983
by the Paperback Division of
W. H. Allen & Co. Ltd
A Howard and Wyndham Company
44 Hill Street, London W1X 8LB

First published in Great Britain by W. H. Allen & Co. Ltd, 1982

Copyright © Jonathan King, 1982

Printed in Great Britain by
Hunt Barnard Printing Ltd., Aylesbury, Bucks.

ISBN 0 352 31308 0

THE BOOK
OF GENESIS

THE BOOK
OF GENESIS

In the beginning there was Jonathan.

Great excitement that Mrs Farting was expecting. On the train from Epsom in the morning, Farting broke the news to Mutsworth and the entire carriage applauded. Rising executives, all on the lower rungs of success but going up fast, packed with ambition.

Farting was doing rather better than the others. His company liked him, believed in him. He was qualified. He was adaptable. He worked long hours and was willing. It's terribly important to be willing. Farting was – above all else – willing. His wife was attractive and friendly. She mixed well with senior executives and their wives, she attended female company get-togethers. And she was willing.

Privately, Mutsworth predicted that Farting was in for big things. Due very soon to be promoted out of the Epsom train. And, indeed, he was. Shortly after the arrival of Jonathan, who took a long time to emerge and was not in the least bit willing, Farting became department head and then assistant to the MD and then Managing Director himself and his shares in the company grew as he and the company did until, with the help of a merchant banker introduced to him by an old school friend, Farting owned the whole operation and was very, very successful indeed. The business was a growing concern, expanding with the economy, perfect in the global market place.

Farting was a millionaire, and no longer in the slightest bit willing. His wife was socially enormously acceptable and not willing either. Jonathan got very little attention but tried very hard and had become exceedingly willing. Jonathan had not been planned. Covertly, Farting blamed him on an ancient prophylactic discovered in the bottom of a drawer.

The Fartings owned a very big mansion in Berkshire and grew race horses. Always the greatest love of both Mr and Mrs Farting, horses dominated their social life, from shows and point to points and hunting and riding to the breeding and training of fine racing machines. Apart from the company, now a conglomerate, Sir and Lady Farting had no greater love, with the possible exception of themselves.

Very early in life, Jonathan had been shown to the horses. As soon as he could toddle, Jonathan had been pushed up to the horses. And one day, a muzzling stallion, drooling horse foam and gluey saliva from a large set of unattractive yellow teeth, had decided it didn't like the smell of baby Jonathan, had concluded that the tiny offering – though white and almost square – was not a cube of sugar, and had done the only sensible thing under the circumstances, kicked baby Jonathan quite a distance with a disdainful hoof.

Babies being essentially rubbery and unbreakable, Jonathan had sustained no physical injury beyond a large purple bruise that caused merriment when displayed by Mrs Farting at parties.

Mentally, however, the effect was catastrophic. Baby Jonathan decided he didn't like horses, howled and screamed whenever brought near them, vomited sick everywhere and eventually would freeze into a terrified state of concrete, trembling numbness.

Mr and Mrs Farting, later to be Sir and Lady Farting and eventually Lord Farting, simultaneously decided they didn't like baby Jonathan and consigned him to

8

a series of nannies and nurses and, finally, to the welcoming arms of boarding school and university.

They also decided they would have no more babies but many more horses.

The Farting household became a peaceful and successful place. Farting lost a lot of his hair, and the rest turned a distinguished grey, but he kept a trim figure by being sensible at eating and by riding a lot. His wife's beauty grew more matronly than sensuous and her deportment on foot and on horseback became the epitome of middle-aged elegance. They never visited the schools, but sent chauffeurs in Daimler limousines to collect and deliver their son to and from the establishments. In the summer a compulsory holiday took them to the Martinez Hotel in Cannes and they toasted their fine bodies at the beach, leaving Jonathan to his own devices, which were not many. He was pushed into parties with children his own age, all of whom rode ponies or horses of some kind and didn't speak to him.

Sir Farting was considered good looking in a gentlemanly way, his wife attractive and well dressed, with not too much make up and very decently styled coiffure.

One day, the Grand National was won by a Farting horse. It was a time for enormous celebration in the household. Swift – a chestnut stallion – romped home ahead of the field leaving hundreds of crushed and broken opponents strewn about the course behind him. Swift was toasted in champagne from the cup itself, and Lady Farting was at one point lifted bodily off the ground by her happy husband and actually bared her ankles in the drama of it all. So wealthy was the Farting Stable that Swift was not sold for stud to another, foreign breeder, but retained to father further Farting champions. The press acclaimed this British nationalism. In due course, Swift poked his mighty organ up a suitable filly and a tiny foal stumbled into the hay with fire in its eye

9

and strength in its legs as it tripped and staggered about to the cooing and aahing of Lady Farting and her inane friends. The baby stallion was named Yahoo and a great future was predicted for him by sports writers and alcoholics alike.

No such luck for Jonathan, generally ignored.

After school, Jonathan went up to university. He had achieved reasonable exam results but his place was granted due to the intercession of the master of his father's old college and possibly facilitated by an enormously generous gift endowed by Lord Farting on the university for vital and urgent refurbishing of lecture rooms.

Jonathan had not been a particularly popular boy at school. He was not pretty enough to interest those attracted by such assets, nor good enough at sports to acquire the attention of masters or prefects. He was no great intellectual, nor creative in arts or sciences. He was incredibly willing, but willingness is no advantage at boarding school. In fact, he was – because of it – considered a weed and ignored. He made no friends at all and went about the daily drudge of work and play with obedience and monotony. The only passion in his life was a vehement and positive hatred of horses. Which guaranteed him no acknowledgment at all from his parents, save a mildly scornful awareness that he existed and an unexpressed desire that he didn't.

It was made clear to Jonathan that, after university, he was on his own. Financially, until that point, he had been considered a small responsibility of Lord Farting's, like life insurance and gardeners. In his last term he had been asked, through a servant, whether he would take a job working with the horses. Upon his declining, no alternative employment was offered, his teddy bears and pyjamas were packed into a trunk and he was informed they were there to be collected upon the termination of his education.

London is a hard city for an out-of-work graduate. Jonathan, with what little funds he had saved from his college allowance, took a small, barely furnished room in Earls Court and attended the labour exchanges. The first job offer came from Selfishes, a giant department store in Regent Street. There was a vacancy in the window dressing section. His interview with Miss Personnel passed uneventfully. She kept taking swigs out of a chipped yellow teacup that smelt distinctly of rubbing alcohol and asked him personal questions about suburban life and commuter train travel, none of which he was capable of answering.

As a result, he got the job.

His immediate boss was a young man called Henry with a complexion of pimples and very lacquered hair. Henry's trousers were rather too tight and his bottom rather too large. He walked with very small steps so as not to cause a rip in the material or a tear in the seams. His windows were not very good since he could not conceivably bend down to alter anything, so from the waist upwards they seethed with colour and design, an extravagance of laces and feathers, wigs and pearls, hats and trees and sunsets of silk.

Jonathan's job was to deal with the lower three or four feet of the windows. Henry was quite explicit in his orders about these areas, but, years ago, had given up all hope of creating art around the knees or ankles and, having decided Jonathan had about as much skill in expressing himself as the average lorry driver, shrugged his lightly built-up shoulders and settled for top heavy beauty in his work.

"How old are you, then, dear?" he asked politely, in a pause needed to draw breath as he sat across an enamel table in the staff canteen.

"Twenty-one," said Jonathan, whose milestone had just passed with no celebration or observance.

"Old enough to know better, darling. The trouble with you is you don't make the best of yourself, dear. I mean – vader that riah! Strings, dear, rats' tails. You're in London now. You must tailor the bonce, honey."

Jonathan found Henry rather difficult to understand but let him ramble on in his soothing, high pitched lisp; hypnotised by the clatter of cutlery and chinaware and the angry buzz of a million gossiping shop girls spitting venom between mouthfuls of yoghourt. The food was virtually inedible. Henry had catalogued it on swishing past, tray in hand. "Afterbirth stew; embryo boiled in port wine; cardboard and glue cheesecake; maggots in blood sauce; goats testicles pickled in mustard, and a bacon sandwich," he'd intoned for the hundredth time. The descriptions fitted the taste rather well. The restaurant stank of carbolic soap and puke and – strangely – shoe polish. Jonathan wondered why.

His fellow minion under Henry was a girl named Gloria. Gloria managed to break things quite easily. She was sharing a flat with five Australian girls who were all working as temps and "making much more money than me but I can't type, see, so I've got to go for the menial jobs like this one which I'd give up in a shot if I could find a fella with money to dominate me and take me away from all this."

Gloria was pretty in a common way, with blunt, round features and dyed brown hair. When she laughed her whole body shook and since she didn't wear a bra and was quite well endowed in the mammary league two giant jellies wobbled and rumbled in front of you. Some of the randier members of the Selfishes' junior staff nudged each other when she walked past, but she had ambitions far above an ordinary boy and dreamed of a Prince Charming who would snatch her away in a luxury car like a red Renault. She was still waiting.

"Eighteen and no luck. Honestly, Jon, do you think I'm past it? My skin's beginning to go. Look." She pulled up her brown knitted jumper to expose a podgy stomach creased with puppy fat wrinkles.

"See. I got a tan in Majorca last year and I think I've got skin cancer now." She pointed at a patch of pigment near her navel, lighter than the rest of her.

"What d'you think, Jon? What d'you think? Come on, you went to university. You learn about things like that there."

Gloria had not been to university. Neither had Henry. This was a source of minor irritation to both of them, but they had converted it into pleasure since Jonathan was the junior of the three and their lack of qualifications had obviously done them no harm at all in the career rat race of big business.

Gloria wore spectacles much too big for her face and looked like a fly of some kind. But she was a happy soul when she wasn't crying and, sometimes, even when she was. Fortunately, neither of them knew about Jonathan's esteemed background. A marked change in their attitude might well have occurred had that happened. Since, therefore, Jonathan appeared to all intents and purposes an inferior being on both their scales of value judgements, they were basically pleasant to him and allowed him to listen to their problems, make them coffee, share their mealtimes and examine their desires.

After a few months at Selfishes, Jonathan began to enjoy himself in a drab, monotonous way. Every morning he would wake at 6:10 to the shrill sound of a Teasmaid kettle hissing steam into the air and hot water into the teapot (a little) and over the floor (a lot). The radio, tuned to Capital 194, would provide a welcome, friendly backdrop of commercials, trite dj dialogue, traffic information he didn't need, community project facts he didn't want and occasional music he didn't like as he blearily collected a grubby towel from a table top coated with dust and wandered down the linoleum-lined corridor to the bathroom, attempting to conceal the morning glory bulge in his stained pyjamas.

He would dress in his jacket, tie and trousers, (compulsory) as he gazed unseeing out on the cold mass of the Earls Court Road, seething with grumpy commuters whose eyelids were gummed with lash dandruff and whose hair could have done with a universal brush.

Slamming the door of his tiny little home and leaving behind it the odour of stale Kentucky Fried Chicken and the tumbled mess of soggy teabags on the floor near the wastebin, he would stumble across the road, narrowly missing death at the hands of blind drivers, and catapault down the grimy steps of the tube station. Four thousand breaths of BO, cigarettes and unchanged socks later, he would emerge into the light of Regent Street like a mole from a sewer and, usually, hang up his jacket behind the door of their miniature office just before the other two arrived.

Henry was normally impeccable except for a dullness in his eyes and a passing yawn. Immediately he would regale them both with tales of his outrageous evening, of boyfriends old and new, of clubs bizarre and wonderful, of adventures sordid and exhilarating. Gloria, snub nose buried deep in a mug of instant coffee, was trying to regain consciousness from a night spent drugged by cheap Australian wine purchased in multi-litre flagons by her flatmates' ill-gotten wealth. Jonathan learnt to say nothing but "really" and "oh" during Henry's morning soliloquies, and soon acquired a method of not listening at all but of contemplating the corridor and waiting for the morning bell to go.

When it went, a bustle of activity heralded the

pending opening hour and life took on its daily hum-drum routine. Since window dressing often needed night time work, the team frequently gathered with other employees and slaved away after the store had closed. In return, days off were granted with unfortunate regularity, and Jonathan found himself sitting in the park, alone, or in a cinema, alone, or in his room, alone. These times were not good times. They were not regulated, coordinated, disciplined times. Jonathan had to make his own entertainment. He preferred working. That also gave him company, since neither Henry nor Gloria thought fit to offer him social benefits.

To compensate for Henry's promiscuous and racy sex-life, Gloria was still, like Jonathan, a virgin. She thought she might be Lesbian, only she didn't fancy girls. She discussed relentlessly with Jonathan whether or not she should have her hymen pierced, not waiting for opinions or answers but speaking for the sake of it.

"Not short of offers, no, but I'd hate to screw up my chances when Mr Right comes along if he thinks I've never been with anyone else and I turn out to have lost it to some scruffy Greek in Harrow. Fat chance I'd have then."

Gloria, deep down inside, was a conventionalist. Her dreams and fantasies involved love, romance and wealth. But she'd be prepared to settle for conformity, marriage, children and drudgery. Not that she ever admitted it. She was proud of the fact that she'd resisted "the physical urge", as she put it.

Henry never resisted "the physical urge" and took joy in flaunting his lusts in front of Gloria, tempting her with tales of butchness and badness, of orgies and mutual masturbation. Henry liked saying dirty things to Gloria and Gloria liked pretending to be shocked. Jonathan was not particularly interested in any of it, but found their dance of depravity mildly diverting when they played it most well. He'd had

15

erections in the mornings from an early age, and discovered sticky patches in his bed soon after, but he found desire hard to acquire and impossible to feed, so he left it alone and got on with working and living and listening.

Soon, however, the peaceful pattern of his life was to be disrupted and shattered.

The halls of Selfishes are not the greatest setting for high drama. The worker bees of the cellars, forever toiling at their tasks, have lowered the ceilings of their ambitions and raised the floors of their depressions so life can continue with reason and sense in an ordered fashion. Jonathan was perhaps never befitted to wear the green apron of permanent drudgery. His childhood had, possibly, stamped upon him unknowingly the seal of individuality. Certainly his genes contained fire, desire, thirst, wonder. Or perhaps he was merely slightly barmy, touched, mad.

Either way, one dark, forbidding evening in the blackened window of Selfishes, Regent Street, London, when quite on his own, with no dirty or disturbing thoughts in his head, Jonathan's life took a twist down an extraordinary side turning.

To put it bluntly – he fell in love.

THE BOOK
OF HOPE

THE BOOK
OF HOPE

Glamour in a shop window is only from the front.
When the spotlights are in place and the clothes are
correctly arranged, a scene of tone and beauty strikes
the passing pedestrian. On a rainy evening, with a
wind lashing umbrellas inside out and gusts of
muddy water exploding up the legs from rushing
tyres, only a glance is awarded the bright, quiet chic
of displayland.

From the back of the window, material is stapled
badly into position; pink cloth bodies peek through
the most undignified areas; shoes are stuffed with
old newspapers -- and all against a backdrop of glaring, reflected light, wet glass, scurrying shapes and
shadows and a lot of noise. Seams in wigs and lad-
ders in nylons abound. The world from the rear is
not the fantasy from the front.

But it was from here, crouched in a corner replacing a bulb, that Jonathan fell in love. He was looking
up to angle the light and he found a face gazing back
at him. Eyes of grey-green with long lashes held his
hypnotised. They spoke peace, quiet, relaxation,
thought. They rejected the howl of theatre traffic
outside and went into the soul, meditating, restful.

From the perfect eyes he saw the perfect nose –
tilted coquettishly – shaped like a dream. Lips regular, skin smooth with a pale pink tinge, cheekbones
high, fine and accented with just a brush of brown
makeup. A haughty face, but a lovely one.

Jonathan had worked with mannequins for months and regarded them as dummies – nothing more nor less. But this one was different. The expression absolutely captured the dignity of lifelessness. She could not have been machine made – the lines of her bones had the mathematical skill of Michelangelo; her flesh breathed like that of David. Standing as she was in a well fitting summer frock, she stood out – the centrepiece of the display. No pins had been needed, no unsightly stuffing. As he looked and changed the angle of the spotlight, her expression altered. An imperceptible smile crept onto her lovely face. Her eyebrows raised slightly in a quizzical fashion. Her chin lifted a fraction and Jonathan swore he could see her cheeks tremble with the air of life.

For a moment he was physically frightened. The adrenalin rushed to his stomach and chilled it like iced acid.

Was someone playing a practical joke? Was this a real woman, smuggled in to disturb his tranquil work and shatter his evening?

He stood up and cautiously moved towards her, prepared for her to burst into life and shout "boo". As he slipped between the light and the mannequin, it changed again, seemed to sigh with relief, to prepare for his embrace. Shoulders relaxed, head lowered, eyes still looking at him but now from below, flirting, coy, twinkling with humour.

Human or dummy? He peered close, couldn't make up his mind. He had seen mimes in stores and on the street with their faces and rigid postures looking less alive than this mannequin. Gingerly, he raised his hand and stretched out a nervous finger, fondling the skin of the cheek. He jumped. It was warm, soft. It gave under his touch.

He laughed. "My God, you had me fooled there," he said.

No movement, no sign returned his embarrassment.

"OK. You win. I fell for it."

Still nothing. He was making a fool of himself. He glanced through the glass. Nobody was paying any attention to the lunatic in the window. Steaks were burning, televisions were waiting, slippers were warming on the hearths of suburbia, and, for now, consciousness was wet trouser turn-ups flapping at the ankles, jets of rain dripping down necks, and the feel of damp material rubbing thighs.

He turned back to the mannequin. Surely she had moved again. Her expression was more serious now, a fraction forbidding, no humour at all. Once more he trembled a digit towards her, watching the eyes for movement, the lashes for a quiver. Nothing.

Yes, warm, soft, but firm – not the flesh of a human body, but also not the waxen shell of a dummy. Growing brave, he felt the nose, lips. Indeed, whilst lacking the cushiony spring of a real face, it was somehow giving, supple.

By now he knew it wasn't a joke. This was no Henry in drag; no Australian friend of Gloria's made up to startle him. This was just another mannequin standing in the middle of a window display, lifeless and manufactured. He ran his fingers down her flawless limbs. Indeed, there was even a little triangular chip in the plastic where an oafish porter had bumped her against some metal corner.

A giant ache of disappointment welled up inside him, as though he had lost a very dear possession. It was a feeling he had never experienced before, and he slumped back down to the floor exhausted by the sensation. Looking up through the jungle of legs and flapping material he saw the dummy watching him. Her face said: "Don't be ridiculous. You didn't really think I was a human being, did you? And why should I be? What advantages do you have over me? Your feet ache, your head aches, your body needs sleep. I'm absolutely happy here – the puppet of a million hands, observing the steady pace of humanity as it rushes past me in the hysteria of existence."

"But you can't breathe or love or hate," Jonathan answered. A pedestrian foolish enough to stop in the storm and gaze into the window would have observed a young man talking to himself.

"Why should I bother, and, anyway, who says I can't?" smiled the mannequin.

She had a point. After all, if she was completely lifeless, why was he having a conversation with her, he thought.

Slowly, he positioned the spotlight and went back into the store. It was his last duty, and he put on the ancient green overcoat purchased at Oxfam and left the building to the surly nod of the security guard. Standing in the drenching rain he peered through the waterfall into the refracted light of the window. As the rain streaked down, her image danced and shifted sensuously.

"Dear me," thought Jonathan as he went home, "how strange. I could have sworn there was more to that mannequin than met the eye." He thought about it all evening, as he swallowed a tasteless Chinese takeaway composed of gristle and monosodium glutamate. Her image remained in his brain as the television newsreader chanted the nasty occurrences of the day. It stayed in his head all night, replacing his usually empty sleep with a spectacular and colourful Busby Berkeley dream routine. It was there as he woke, as he washed, and as he dressed. To him, it was curious. To others, it would have seemed insane. In fact, Jonathan strange as it may sound, had indeed, fallen in love.

Some days later Jonathan became aware that something was wrong. He made excuses to wander into the window. He sat just outside it during his tea-break. He felt himself wondering how life was different for a model. One time he even hypnotised himself into a robot-like stupor and frightened Gloria who thought he was having a fit. He put a few fragile questions to Henry: Didn't he think that mannequin was more graceful, more natural than most of the others? "Not particularly," came the answer, "hand me some more pins, dear." At night, disturbed by the relentless one track of his imagination, he found sleeping difficult, and began to be late for work, arriving unshaven and crumpled and – according to Henry – generally smelly.

After weeks of this obsession, Jonathan decided he had to confide in somebody. His first instinct was to turn to Gloria, who at least occasionally listened during her speeches, but eventually decided that Henry was a man of the world, older, experienced. He would neither be shocked nor confused by the information.

Accordingly, one lunchtime in the canteen, Henry selected diarrohea soup followed by sliced roast foot and pureed boils, and pirouetted towards a red-topped table enamelled in grime. Jonathan followed him discreetly, sat opposite and tried to introduce himself into the conversation.

This Herculean task proved nearly impossible. At one point, having edged towards the subject inch by inch, – he said: "Henry, I need your advice. I've fallen in love with a mann. . . "

Henry burst in, "My dear, at last! Congratulations. I know it's worrying you at the moment, but I can assure you everything will turn out fine. Now tell me, dear, has this little affair been consummated yet?"

"No, Henry. Not a man – a mannequin. That one in the window. You know, the one I keep pointing out to you."

"What? Don't be ridiculous, dear. You don't mean *love*. You mean physical attraction. To you, that dummy symbolises your ideal lover. Nothing wrong there. Find the girl that looks similar to her, and, don't forget, it's probably *my* creation of make-up and clothes that you've *actually* fallen for, and I don't blame you, darling. Flip through a few copies of *Tatler* and you'll see a million identical girls – I *hope!* Personally, I suspect they intentionally fashion themselves on my designs, but either way, honey, there are thousands of clones from my fingertips out there in deb-land.''

Jonathan went no further. He knew he could not explain to Henry, who burbled on about his art and creations, turning the conversation happily back to himself and ignoring Jonathan's unhappy wrigglings. So, the next day, Jonathan took his teabreak with Gloria and told her, in the privacy of a quiet employees' stairwell, his horrid secret.

Gloria was quite shocked. ''Are you all right in the head? You can't fall in love with an inanimate object.'' She pronounced it ''inaminate.''

''Look, Jon, that's not love. That's fantasy. You can't let fantasy rule your life.'' She took his hand, being quite motherly. ''I think you better go out and get your rocks off. I think you better go out and throw it up some bird in the Lyceum. Why don't you come out with us one night? Tracy's going down to the Best Disco next Tuesday. Come along and let yourself go. Love for a dummy! Whatever next! What do you do with her in bed, love? How are you going to take her out to nice restaurants? How's she going to earn a living and drive a car and buy a house and do all the things you want a girl to do? Give over, it's just frustration, love, nothing serious.''

It seemed no one would take his problem seriously. So Jonathan gave up his miniature attempt at communication, and allowed his fetish to grow quietly in the tissue of his mind, like cancer. He even consented to being dragged along to the Lyceum, a beautiful theatre just off the Strand, desecrated by flashing neon globes, cell-crushing decibels of disco music, drunk youths with acned cheeks and an overwhelming odour of hot dogs and onions. One of the Australian girls danced with him, trod on his foot, pushed a tongue the size of a tuna fish down his throat and almost poisoned him with breath heavily flavoured with stale tobacco and rum and Coke. Jonathan found it impossible to perform the required physical functions.

Even Henry persuaded him to accompany him on a debauched visit to the Catacombs, a sleazy gay club in Earls Court which thronged with butch motor cyclists in black leather and silver chains who adopted masculine poses and had chunks of cucumber stuffed down their trousers. Strangely, Jonathan felt safer there than he did at the Lyceum.

Weeks turned into months and the hidden hand of Walt Disney coloured the grey landscape with a splash of blue and green and yellow until spring gave birth to early summer. Every day Jonathan gazed at the mannequin. As displays changed, so did her hairstyle, her skin tones, her wardrobe, her setting, her companions. At weekends and evenings he stood in front of her window and allowed the two of them to merge into one – inside and outside – living and statue – man and mannequin.

The news, when it reached him, was a shock, but not unpleasant. Lord Farting had been killed jumping a fence on his prize hurdler, Yahoo. Lady Farting, rushing to his assistance, had suffered a crushed skull as the rearing horse ungratefully lashed out an accusing hoof. Jonathan, the only son, due to an absence of will, received millions and millions of pounds in stocks, shares, estates, property, and hard cash. In fact, overnight he became one of the five richest men in Great Britain.

This didn't mean very much to Jonathan, who rather lacked imagination. He shrugged his shoulders and continued life. But the world would not allow such stoicism. Companies needed decisions, the media needed stories, and Jonathan's need for peace and quiet was secondary to those weighty demands. Phones shrilled all over London: newspapers carried stories headed "Shop boy inherits millions" and "Today – the everyday duties of Selfishes' window. Tomorrow – the board room!"

Henry and Gloria behaved very strangely. All of a sudden they looked at him as though he had begun to exist. In one swoop he was more important to them than they were to themselves – a staggering achievement. Their conversation was normally preceded by a clearing of the throat or an adjustment of hair or clothing. His aura had become fragile, delicate. Even a mispronounced word might irritate him or damage them in his eyes. They were, after all, his closest personal friends.

The voyage to the Catacombs became a memorable night of magic to Henry, told in hushed whispers, an exclusive tale for the ears of only his very dearest acquaintances. It was just one example of the many times that he, Henry, and dear Lord Farting (as he now was in Henry's eyes) had ventured out into the world together. Soon, every adventure Henry had ever exaggerated was originally performed in company with Jonathan.

Gloria had almost lost her virginity to Jonathan. They were that close, love. Marriage was on the cards. From a rather plain workmate to be utilised, victimised, ignored or talked at, Jonathan had become that elusive ideal man Gloria was waiting for.

Mr Gross summoned Jonathan to his office in a grovelling, obsequious fashion. Miss Personnel was already there in the corner, rubbing her hands together, beads of pure alcohol decorating her brow. Mr Gross was the big boss, the manager of the entire store. He was very thin and wiry and wore very smart three piece suits in a pin stripe material not available to the men's tailoring department. His teeth were even but yellow and he constantly picked them

26

with a splintered wooden stick. If anyone got close enough, his mouth odour drowned the splash of Aqua Velva patted at dawn on his smooth cheeks. His hair was slicked back in mid-fifties style – blacker than nature intended, and thinning.

It was not generally known that on Wednesdays, early closing, Mr Gross took his briefcase to an address in Soho and dressed up as a prostitute, strolling the streets until the time came to catch his train from Waterloo back to his wife and kids in suburbia. This was Mr Gross' only outgoing occupation. All the rest of the week he remained the efficient, if tacky, general manager of Selfishes and the kind, if distant, husband and father.

"Em – Farting," he said, clearing his throat. "I fear we'll be losing you soon."

Jonathan was by now aware that this event was inevitable.

"I suppose so, sir. I'll be sorry to go. I've been very happy here."

"Well, we've been very happy with you and we'll be sorry to lose you as an employee but not, we hope, as a future customer. Please always remember if there's anything at all we can do for you, just ask."

Miss Personnel grimaced and grinned and twisted her hands until a litre of whisky ebbed from the pores.

"Here is my card – er – Farting," said Gross. "Just in case – some little delicacy – you never know. We may be number two, but you'll always be number one!"

He managed a smile, which made him look like a wolf. A brain wave struck Jonathan. It was, he later remembered, a sensation similar to St Paul's experience on the road to Damascus. A blinding revelation, simple in its concept, far-reaching in its consequences.

"There is one thing, sir."

Mr Gross leant forward, straining to lap up every

knighted syllable and every golden vowel that might drop from the lips of this contact to wealth. Miss Personnel bent towards him until she nearly toppled over like an empty vessel.

"Could I purchase one of the mannequins from Display? It would be a marvellous momento of my happy days here."

Roget's Thesaurus could not have revealed more alternatives to affirmative. "Of course, by all means. Yes, indeed." Mr Gross virtually swallowed his desk in his willingness to subscribe to this unusual but welcome request. Miss Personnel nodded and beamed and exuded pungent vapours. Gross picked up his phone and barked explicit orders at everyone who answered. The ultimate responsibility was given to Henry. Then, with expressions of sorrow, pleasure, anticipation, and gratitude the duo shook farewell to Jonathan's uneasy hand.

Henry had already taken the dummy out of display and had her draped in a flowing robe of yellow velveteen. She dominated the tiny room.

"I must admit, dear, she is a bit special. No trouble at all in remembering the one you meant, you'll notice, honey. There's a twinkle in her eye and a touch of class in her deportment." Henry was terribly nice to Jonathan these days.

Gloria also rallied to the mannequin's defence. "What a lovely thought, to take one of our little treasures home to remember Selfishes by. Still, you won't forget us, will you, love? I mean, she is quite beautiful, but she won't give you the sort of friendship we'll give you, will she, love?"

"Oh, no," Jonathan assured them, his feelings for the model were quite different to his feelings for Henry and Gloria.

They gingerly and politely wrapped the lady in brown paper and carried her through the corridors to the waiting limousine now permanently at Jonathan's disposal.

"Oo – that's lovely," said Gloria, ogling the vehicle.

"Mm – nice," said Henry, casting a discerning eye over the smart, uniformed young chauffeur.

"Yes, a touch of class," echoed Jonathan, watching the mannequin climb delicately, with a little help, into the back of the Rolls Royce.

You could say this was the point where Jonathan crossed the line between sanity and madness. Perhaps it was the sudden and unexpected acquisition of wealth which tipped the balance. Money has provoked strange reactions. Anyway, suddenly the objective, impersonal observation of the mannequin was not enough. Jonathan had seen the changes that money could bring. He'd seen attitudes alter with the publication of the inheritance story. People he thought he'd known well transformed into wholly different beings.

Given the unusual circumstances, that he was obsessed by a shop window dummy manufactured solely for the purpose of display, it seemed to him a logical step to try to breathe life into the body.

There was no point in telling Jonathan to search for an identical shape containing a living, breathing human being. You might just as well have told a healthy young man in love with an unattainable girl to find her double and make do with her. Jonathan worshipped the ground the mannequin stood on. Unpropelled by physical lust, her lack of soft breast tissue or gaping lower orifices mattered not one jot. Symbolising peace, gentility, perfection, stillness, he had discovered in her his Holy Grail, and all that was needed was for her to possess the basic essentials of life to give Jonathan permanent and lasting happiness.

Accordingly, he began to liquidate his inherited assets in order to provide himself with as much immediate cash as possible. To the howls of indignant brokers and shareholders; to the anguish of fellow directors, company lawyers, accountants, and executives; to the hysteria of media and unconnected observers and to the self-righteous bursts of deflation from unions and employees, he closed and sold factories, merged distributors, got rid of valuable stock and behaved in a totally irresponsible fashion.

The results were astronomical. Faced by such lack of intelligent behaviour, the market became confused. Values tripled, profits escalated. Where Jonathan, guided by the good sense and learned counsel of his paid advisors, might have remained merely rich, Jonathan, motivated by insanity, made billions and billions of unexpected extra pounds. In short, virtually overnight he became one of the five richest men in the world.

There are many people who make money by astutely observing the actions of well-informed, shrewd moguls. Sometimes, these financial parasites do not realise they are themselves forming the foundation stones of the empires they are watching. So hundreds of would-be tycoons imitated Jonathan's actions and inflated the value of his decisions.

He was living back in Farting Castle. He kept well away from the nearby stables but was unable to dispose of them due to an ownership trust. His lawyers assured him the stables would eventually belong to him when the complex investigation was over. Out of limited respect for his late parents, he allowed his minions to toss funds in the direction of the trainers and stable managers, so the horses did not actually die of malnutrition or seize up through lack of exercise (though, secretly, he would have been quite happy if they had). He instructed that no contact whatsoever was to take place between home and horses.

He lived in enormous comfort, with the mannequin installed in the main bedroom, to the curiosity of inquisitive staff. Eventually they regarded this eccentricity as merely a minor madness and shrugged their collective shoulders, accustomed by now to weird behaviour amongst the aristocracy.

They never saw his trysts at night, when he sat on the bed and spoke softly for some hours to the motionless figure. And they weren't aware of the plots he was making and the schemes he was hatching to bring the dummy to life.

Farting Castle was a magnificent pile, once owned by Norman dukes and Elizabethan barons. The driveway that led to it from the winding roads cascading off the M6 was almost a mile long, weaving past vast oaks and green lawns. The edifice itself was proud and haughty in weather-beaten stones hundreds of years old. There was a lodge with an archway that gave onto a courtyard. The entrance was massive and imposing, a carved doorway of gremlins and hobgoblins battling unicorns for no good reason. Lord and Lady Farting had been most proud of the status symbol. They had used only a few of the rooms, but often showed visitors from America or the Gulf the spacious wings and corridors with expressions of felicity that, thanks to the enormous success of the business, they had no need to let in the "public" – a word pronounced in the same tone as "leprosy" or "syphilis."

At night the building loomed on the horizon, back lit by the full moon, an orgasm of turrets and spires. An observer standing on the acre of perfectly manicured grass in front of the house would have seen pale light filtering through the damask curtains of the great room on the first floor. There, pacing back and forth in his father's silk dressing gown (rather too long for him), was Jonathan, collecting his thoughts in the presence of his loved one.

He had decided that the solution lay with the intellectuals. In his time at university, Jonathan had been deeply impressed by the control academics possessed over their pupils. They, if anyone, breathed life into the dead tomes of Sophocles and Shake-speare; the philosophies of Sartre and Jung; the theories of Einstein and Freud. He'd never been able to grasp any of them, but those eminent, brainy professors had understood all. They were the vessels of knowledge, the fountains of wisdom. Governments came to them for help and assistance. Who better to tell him how to discover the secret of life? The wonderful world of words, sacred and beckoning from his college days, called to him now. If anywhere, there lay the answer.

Henry came to stay at Farting Castle. He had pointed out to Jonathan that he was due holiday and would love to come and examine the estate. He arrived on the doorstep in a pink satin suit with a white shirt composed mainly of frills and lace, looking like a debauched Lord Fauntleroy – dressed for the part, as he squealed to Jonathan. Servants fell over themselves with amusement. Such blatant caricatures very rarely ventured out of town, and poor country folk had little chance to observe the habits of these rare birds. Soon Henry began to feather his nest and the younger male members of staff discovered the small distance between laughter and seduction was more easily bridged than they had ever conceived possible.

Jonathan took Henry into his confidence. Did he consider that a trip to university might achieve the results? Henry was down to earth but optimistic.

"I mean, let's face it, darling, the entire proposal is preposterous when you analyse it. But, then, impossible things have been done before now. And, if you're determined to give a shot to this extraordinary venture, I suppose a visit to the seat of learning will either show you the whole thing is ridiculous or else give you a clue as to what to do next." Privately, Henry suspected a quick session with a psychiatrist would sort out the problem, but, since society had been suggesting for years that his own habits could be cured in a similar way, he was understandably not eager to propose such a route.

Accordingly, one morning the two of them braved the savage luxuries of the back of the Farting limousine and swept off towards Cambridge. Henry spent most of the drive chatting animatedly to the chauffeur so Jonathan was able to indulge in the pleasures of contemplation and imagination, and they arrived surprisingly quickly. The venerable walls of Peterhouse and the vast quadrangle of Kings sent shivers down his spine and brought back the simple memories of his student days. "How innocent I was then," he thought. "How unaware of the complex passions of the world."

Trinity College is set on the banks of the river Cam, its tall gates surmounted by a stone King Henry clutching a chair leg and observing the relentless stream of spotty and bristly young men below.

Leaving the car parked illegally in the exclusive area in front of the lodge, and slipping a couple of notes into the hands of an obsequious porter, who remembered him from earlier years and had treated him like offal throughout his undergraduate career, Jonathan strolled with Henry under the arch into the huge green square, which smelled of damp moss and burnt toast. While his companion was concentrating on not snapping his ankles on the slippery cobbles as he tottered along in his built up heels, Jonathan allowed the suppressed breaths of adolescence to sweep into his lungs. They were heading for the most learned don in the entire university, the highly respected lecturer in philosophy, Sir Newton Bean.

Sir Newton had rooms in a small courtyard behind the dining room; a quiet, melancholy, shady square of arches and pillars and uneven stones. His name was painted in fading brown letters on a darker brown background. The degree of clarity of the plaque announced who was old and established and important and who was new and bright and garish and on trial. Sir Newton was immensely privileged by having rooms in Neville's Court almost next to the Trinity Library itself.

Even Henry, dampened by the atmosphere of study and intellect, was silent and only whispered when he spoke. Winding upwards on mildewed steps worn down by the feet of generations of scholars, they arrived at a solid oak door and tapped with timidity and fear. Jonathan had called for an appointment, but he knew the punctuality of academics and almost hoped for a silent reaction to his tap. It was not to be. A voice said "enter" and, pushing the heavy barrier open, they found themselves in the presence.

Sir Newton furnished his den through usage rather than design. Books were piled up in every corner, shelves creaked to their weight, they propped tables and occupied chairs. There was a smell of paper and cardboard and leather and dried binding glue. To lessen this odour, Sir Newton had employed the services of tobacco and puffed clouds of smoke towards them from a huge pipe that hung stained and knotted from his mouth.

Sir Newton was all forehead. A giant expanse of brow, trimmed with a few strands of white hair like a moth-eaten ermine. He looked like a bleached tadpole.

Perched on his angular nose were a pair of pre-war tin spectacles, battered through age. The creases on his face were yellow with nicotine and his thin lips had the bluish tinge of heart trouble. He wore a baggy tweed jacket with bulging pockets, and behind the door hung a gown orange with age and dotted with holes burnt by falling cinders. But through this careless tangle of disinterest shone a pair of clear, bright eyes, sparkling with intelligence and merriment, like diamonds in the face of a lizard.

"Farting, isn't it? How are you, boy? Finding life

full of problems, what? Who's this with you? Fashion designer? Hairdresser?"

Henry looked offended and Jonathan hastily introduced him as a friend and colleague from work.

"Well, sit down, sit down. Don't mind the books. They're just as happy on the floor."

Jonathan cleared a couple of chairs and they perched uncomfortably as he explained his dilemma to the old man.

Sir Newton listened keenly. Every now and then he would knock out his pipe (on his shoe, all over the worn and grimy but once very valuable carpet), refill it and suck deeply on the stem as clouds of white fog billowed from the bowl.

The story seemed to take longer than Jonathan had thought it would. He explained his first feelings, his gradually increasing obsession, his desire to breathe life into this shell of beauty. As he talked, he saw even Henry was becoming aware of the depth of his emotions and the sense behind his madness. The old man never interrupted, just puffed away and gazed at the ceiling.

When he'd finished there was a long pause as Sir Newton Bean gathered his interpretation together. Then, clearing his throat, he launched into the following dissertation.

"For centuries philosophers have examined the question of life. Its purpose, its form, its shape. There have been those who consider that every object, human or otherwise, is a projection of an essence, concealed no doubt in a giant museum in the sky. You are aware, I'm sure, of the theories of Pythagoras and of the complex ideas of such new, modern thinkers as Sartre. I won't go into the wealth of thought on the matter with you, here, now. Besides, I personally feel the key lies not with the ashes of old, dead minds but with your own active, living attitudes.

"You must examine your reasons for wishing to transfer to this chosen symbol the abilities already existing in millions of moving, breathing creatures. And then you must question yourself on vital matters with honesty and the probing of a tutored brain."

Sir Newton shifted in his chair with a crackle of parchment and a rasp of dry manuscript. He inhaled deeply on his pipe and blew a vast spiral of smoke into the air.

"What is the ratio between right and wrong? When can we be said to be truly aware of ourselves? The only path to deep knowledge is along the wooded passageways of literature. Consume the Bhagavad Gita and you may find wisdom of many kinds. Wander the poems of Omar Khayyam and magic impulses will stir your sleeping skills. Walk hand in hand with the works of Dickens and Shakespeare and pure analysis of their words will show you the depths of your own abilities.

"Are they dead? Do they cease to be, these giants of forests, these heros of the trees? Can you tell me that, when mere mortal breath ceased to wheeze in their decrepit lungs, the soul and spirit of such mighty artists evaporated into the sky? Look around you, young man. Grasp the proposals of Goethe, the signs of Plato, the legacies of Tolstoy and Rousseau and Coleridge."

He wriggled his legs and wrinkled his brow. The atmosphere of knowledge was aromatic and tranquillising.

"Define life. Define the kind of existence you want for your guinea pig."

Jonathan opened his mouth to reply but the question was obviously rhetorical because Sir Newton Bean went on:

"It is so hard to say for certain what is and what is not. Am I? Are you? Is he?"

He gestured towards Henry, who obviously was not, as his attention had blatantly wandered.

36

"Is that? Is this? Are those," he pondered, pointing at various objects around the study. "We could go on asking forever, before we found an answer. Oh, for sure, many brilliant thinkers have considered that they have, by detailed examination and relentless experiment, come to the ultimate definition. They may even be right. For themselves. Or for us. Or in general. But then again they may not be. This is the calculation we all must make."

He paused once more to suck on the chewed wooden briar and sighed as though all the problems of the universe had descended on his shoulders many years ago, when he was still a young man.

"I digress. Perhaps the vital thing is not assessment, but action. It is action you are seeking, right? Not the frothy opinions of an old fool, buried deep in wisdom, too subjective to realise the problems of others."

He chuckled with an asthmatic hiss and grimaced at his own self-effacement.

"To *do* something, you must first find the source. You must uncover the trickle of water that is the start of the fountain, deep in the hills of knowledge, miles from civilised behaviour, crossing burning deserts of scepticism and surviving battles and wars of hatred. You will be called a fool, a clown, a lunatic, but your only hope is to chart the map of philosophy until you come to the central core of all thinking. This is not an easy journey. Many roads will lead in conflicting directions. Many signposts will have been turned around by the hands of history. The truth is an evasive virgin, constantly running from those who seek her. But I think you are on the right track. You know the route lies in the country of intellect. That is a start. Gather your forces and read acres of print, millions of tomes, thousands of theories. Select well, choose who to believe and who to discard. Good luck, Childe Roland, and beware potholes in the road."

Henry had gone into some kind of coma. His eyes had glazed over and his hair had collapsed like a badly cooked souffle, hanging in lacquered abandon over one eye. Jonathan nudged him to get him out of the trance. The overpowering fragrance of the pipe and the weighty vibrations of a million books had combined with the hypnotic drone of Sir Newton Bean's lecture to conquer time and make all his anxious worries seep away. But now Sir Newton had stopped and Jonathan realised to his sadness that the old man had solved no problems, provided no answers. Still the eyes twinkled brightly through the smoke, implying intellectual awareness that Jonathan could never reach. Looking at Sir Newton, you felt sure he knew everything, saw beyond the facts, held in his brain the secrets of life. Perhaps he just couldn't or wouldn't communicate those wonders. Or perhaps, beneath it all, the veneer of sophisticated knowledge covered an emptiness as hollow as Jonathan's.

"Well, sir, you've been very kind and enormously helpful," he said, getting up and realising he was quite cramped. "I shall put your theories to practical use as soon as I can." He nudged Henry again, who fluttered to life like a butterfly and began adjusting his crowning glory with anxious fingers.

"There is one more thing, young man," said Sir Newton, unwinding his body and standing up like the caterpillar in Alice getting off the mushroom.

"Yes, sir?" said Jonathan, holding his breath. Was this the moment he'd been waiting for? Was this – encapsulated – the ultimate aphorism of wisdom that would give him at least a clue to his solution?

"Are you driving back through London? And, if so, would you be so kind as to give me a lift?"

"Er – yes, we are, as it happens. Of course, you'd be most welcome. . ."

The further Sir Newton got from his study, the more out of place he looked. He put on a new purple overcoat which did not fit him at all well and made him look like a maggot emerging from a plum. He picked up a walking stick and popped a brown trilby on his head.

The three of them shuffled out into the courtyard. Passing undergraduates saluted or nodded as he wobbled along between Jonathan and Henry, who had to slow their pace and shorten their step to an agonising rate. Other dons smiled or frowned or merely strode on, college workers fawned and grovelled. It took an interminable time to reach the car. Sir Newton rambled on about university gossip, faculty politics and obscure romantic poets. He was dreadfully impressed by the Rolls Royce and insisted on sitting by the window and waving at people as they cruised down Kings Parade towards the A10. He spent at least five minutes making them hold their breath so he could hear the clock ticking. Then he slumped back, stretching a pair of worn Hush Puppies out in front of him, and lit his pipe which had gone out during the expedition from room to car, although it had never been removed from his mouth. Jonathan began to wonder if it was actually a part of his body.

When they reached the outskirts of town, Sir Newton asked whether they might kindly drop him off at a tiny bookshop in the Charing Cross Road. "A wonderful place, full of the most obscure publications. Do you know, once I discovered there an original first edition of the great *Don Juan* by Lord Byron, the clubfoot romantic who so dominated all of our adolescent dreams. Ah, romance, chivalry! You cannot imagine, Farting, the sheer pleasure of holding in your hand a bound volume which was almost certainly once clutched by the writer himself! A mere collection of paper sheets, you think. A few printed words gathered together in a leather and card sleeve. But, no! The ideas, the emotions, the sensations of experience that flow from the phrases and sentences written by those geniuses actually convey themselves physically up one's fingers into one's blood."

He was getting quite excited, the fire of learning burning bright in his body. Jonathan was pleased to be able to wave goodbye to him at the corner of Charing Cross Road. Henry slumped back in his seat.

"My dear, I'm absolutely exhausted! I never would have believed somebody could be so boring. I thought a visit to Cambridge would be a fabulous parade of beauties in gowns and caps. Well, I'm sorry – but I'm never going *there* again. Once is quite enough, darling, I'm sure you agree."

Sadly, Jonathan *did* agree. The journey had not proved a success. They were back to square one. The mannequin was no nearer life than it had been that morning.

Sir Newton Bean waited until the limousine was out of sight and then walked purposefully in the opposite direction to the bookshop. It was not generally known that every now and then on Wednesday afternoons Sir Newton Bean took his pipe and walking stick to the streets of Soho, where he frequently met a pretty young transvestite and indulged in acts of heavy petting until the time came to catch his train to Cambridge and the solemn dignity of his book-lined study at Trinity College.

Jonathan was so depressed on the ride back to Berkshire that Henry forgot to chat to the chauffeur and found himself immersed in cheering his friend up.

"Perhaps he just wasn't the right wise man, dear," he said, crossing his elegant legs with a wince. "Perhaps you'll find a nice intellectual at Oxford."

"No, the whole thing's crazy. I don't know why I'm bothering. I think I'll just sell up and go live somewhere else in the sun."

Henry twitched and cleared his throat.

"No, you don't want to do that, dear. You've got

to persevere for a bit, if you're serious about it. I think you should go and see a doctor, darling. Look, they're transplanting hearts and lungs and all *kinds* of organs from one corpse to another these days with the most sensational results. Surely a surgeon can breathe life into a mannequin if anybody can!"

Jonathan looked thoughtful but interested and Henry pressed on, delighted to have found a subject to cheer up his benefactor.

"Just you let me nose about and track down a wizard in the world of medicine, honey. I'll check out who's the tops and then we'll mince along and see whether we can get any sense out of the man."

He paused and allowed his fingertips to caress a particularly nasty pimple which had sprouted white-headed at the end of his prominent nose.

"The only problem is, sweet," he said, realising that Jonathan had crossed the line from hopelessness to optimism and was in fine mood to discuss Henry's future, "I can't take too much more time off from Selfishes. That Mr Gross, dear, has become a *tyrant* since you left. A *tyrant*! I'm expected to do windows that have never been done before! Honestly, I reckon he'll be getting me doing displays in the basement soon, to enthrall the staff on their way to stock! It's the shock of you going, darling, that's done it. He had great faith in you, Jonathan, dear."

Mr Gross had hardly hear of Jonathan before Miss Personnel had brought the unfortunate family accident to his attention.

Henry paused again and made certain the sound proofed glass partition between driver and employer was well and truly in position. Personal matters should never be discussed in front of junior staff, he firmly believed.

"My holiday's all up and I can't keep asking for time off, so I can only really check out the Harley Street barons during lunch hours and, you know, I *must* eat, magic, to keep the strength up and the

41

beauty vibrant." He preened himself, amused by his ability to self mock.

Jonathan was not really paying attention. His mind was elsewhere, analysing the prospects of life being supplied medically rather than intellectually. Henry's problems seemed remote to him at present.

Henry cleared his throat with a sound like a bantam laying an egg and stroked a stiffly lacquered lock (he carried a miniature portable spray in his comb pocket at all times) back into place.

"Are you listening to me, Miss Farting?" he barked, accustomed to being appreciated and not ignored.

"What, oh, sorry, Henry, yes, yes, that does seem a sensible idea."

"Of course it's a sensible idea, baby, but who's going to track down the right man for the job? Not you, dear. You're hardly a connoisseur of medics, are you? I'd *love* to do it for you, but as I said," and he raised his voice to make sure Jonathan was listening this time, acquiring a steely quality that defied inattention, "I'm finding it very hard to get time off from Selfishes."

"Oh, dear," said Jonathan.

Henry looked despairing during the pause that followed. Was he going to have to put the thought into words or was Jonathan capable of being led to it himself?

"Trying to discover an effective solution to your problem is virtually a fulltime job, honey," he snapped.

"I know, it is, isn't it? Sometimes I feel as though I have taken on an impossible task, a heavy burden. I do cherish your help and support, Henry. When do you have to go back to work?"

"Pretty soon, I'm afraid. And when that moment comes, I really won't be able to help you anymore."

Beads of sweat were beginning to stand out on Henry's forehead, between the spots. This mental effort was exhausting him. One large globe dropped from his face and plopped dark and wet onto the thick beige lambswool rug. He was not normally a subtle person, and the role of Machiavelli did not come easy to him. Somehow he did not appear to be getting his message through. Sighing, he wiped his brow and came straight out with it.

"Why don't you make me an offer to come and work for you, darling, as a sort of personal assistant, you know, taking the pressure from you, investigating potential boffins, keeping the body snatchers at bay. I'm very good at that kind of thing."

Jonathan raised his eyebrows. He still regarded Henry as his superior and couldn't quite relate to this reversal of roles. But, on the other hand, why not?

"That's a good idea. But what about your career – all the years you've spent building up a reputation?"

Henry sighed and placed a hand on his breast, like Hamlet suffering unspeakable pains.

"It would be difficult. Might even be impossible. But I feel you *need* me, honey, and there's nothing that touches me more than a cry from a virgin heart. Here's little you, innocent, naive, searching for a Holy Grail. Perhaps I could help your quest. Surely that is motive enough for a girl?"

"Well, could you afford to do it? I mean retirement schemes and pension plans and insurance and mortgage and all that?"

Henry looked hurt. "I'm not that old yet, dear! Quite a young chicken underneath the panstick. No, seriously, you'd have to help me a teeny weeny bit financially, you know, guarantee me a decent sum that I could put by and whisk me onto the payroll of one of the companies. You're not exactly impoverished, honey."

"What sort of money do you think would compensate. . .?" asked Jonathan, with genuine curiosity.

"Well, taking into account my position at Selfishes

and all that, I could *probably* cope if you gave me a hundred thousand to stick in the bank and a thousand a week after tax as salary."

Jonathan looked amazed. "Isn't that an awful lot?"

"Well, if you're going to be like that dear. . ." muffled Henry, pouting petulantly. "I'm only suggesting it as a favour to you. *I'm* doing fine where I am. . ."

Next day Henry was driven to Selfishes where he handed in his notice to Mr Gross and Miss Personnel with the minimum of fuss and the maximum of pleasure.

"There's a young lady to see you, sir."

From the disapproving sound of the butler's voice, Jonathan knew this was not a high society woman of his mother's class. He strongly disliked the butler, who – every day – seemed to silently convey the indisputable fact that he was not his father's son. Jeeves, as he was privately nicknamed between Jonathan and Henry, believed in the old order of things. And Jonathan had a sneaking suspicion that Jeeves, deep down inside, had a closet admiration for horses.

"Show her in."

An extraordinary spectacle staggered into the drawing room, tripping on the carpet and almost falling on her face. Her hair was tinted and bleached into a basic red and green with streaks of yellow. Down one side of her face was a slash of lipstick like a Frankenstein scar. Her eyes were dipped in mascara and looked as though she was auditioning for a part as a koala bear. She wore skintight satin red pants and high stiletto heels on glittering day-glo shoes. Her ample bosom thrust out the front of a T-shirt proclaiming "Sid Vicious is dead" underneath a new and shiny black leather jacket. Gloria had gone punk.

"Hello, love, how are you doing?" she asked, fumbling for a chair. "Me contact lenses aren't ready yet and glasses don't really go with the outfit. Still, let's 'ave a look and see how you are."

She dragged her bumble bee specs out of a tiny gold bag and was instantly transformed into the usual – if a trifle altered – Gloria.

"I'm fine, Gloria. What's happened to you, then? Why the change in style?"

"Well, love, I got fed up with the same old look and Tracy – you remember Tracy, my Australian friend – dared me to go punk so I did and here I am."

Jonathan gaped at the vision, at a loss for words.

"Well, what do'you think? And aren't you pleased to see me, then?"

He shook himself awake and got up and gave her a brotherly kiss.

"Of course I am. I've missed you dreadfully. How did you get out here?"

"Came by bus. Dreadful journey, love."

"I should think it was. I don't think the locals have experienced too much punk rock in person out here."

"I've got me case in the hall. Is it all right if I stay a few days? 'Cause I've walked out of Selfishes and I'm desperate to get out of the flat. The girls are entertaining Swedish sailors all this week and they all keep repeating themselves 'cause they can't understand each other!"

"You're very welcome. I'll get Jeeves to prepare you a room."

"Jeeves?!"

"Oh, that's what we call the butler. He was that rather snooty man who ushered you in."

Gloria sprawled out in the chair, an elegant Louis XIV number, her legs stretched over the carpet and her arms hanging down.

"I'm shattered, love. Can't take any more."

"Why did you leave Selfishes?"

"Oh, they didn't like the punk look. So I told them to stuff it."

"The department must be rather depleted. You know Henry's not coming back after his holiday?"

"Yes, love, he told me. He's working for you! What a turn up for the books. That'll teach him manners!" She giggled.

Jonathan ordered tea, which arrived on his parents' delicate bone china service, and they strolled out onto the lawn. It was a glorious May evening. The sun was out and the view over most of Berkshire was breathtaking. He explained his quest, which made Gloria rather irritated.

"I don't know why you bother, love, really I don't. Find a nice girl and settle down, that's my advice to you. This other obsession will lead to madness. You mark my words, it'll end in tears!"

"Gloria, I'm determined to give it a try. Now – not another word of pessimism if you value our friendship."

Jonathan was not usually so definite and Gloria was quite overawed by his attitude, so she shrugged her shoulders and looked at her toes.

That evening, as Jonathan showed her the room she was to occupy and left her to tidy up for dinner, he found himself wandering along one of the corridors in the servant quarters when he heard raised voices and a door flew open beside him, catapulting a flustered Henry into his arms.

"Henry! Whatever are you doing?"

The door had slammed closed again and the corridor was silent except for the two of them recovering their breath after the collision.

"Oh, hello darling. Just been having a word or two with the chauffeur about servicing the Rolls. It really was running very strangely on the way back from town today. I'm sure that man hasn't been topping up the oil – naughty boy!"

"Gloria's with us," said Jonathan, expecting joy from his surprise news.

"Cunning bitch," said Henry under his breath. "Oh, wonderful, honey. Just like old times, isn't it?"

"Well, not really. Have you seen her since she went punk?"

"No, dear, we've only spoken on the phone. Looks a bit odd, does she? Attractive at all?"

"Good God, no – monstrous. Quite funny in a derivative sort of way. But don't tell her I said so. She's very sensitive at the moment – lost her job, you know."

"Really. Well, we'd better put her up for a day or two, I suppose."

Henry did not appear to be as excited by the presence of their friend as Jonathan had anticipated. But, then, he was like that. Unwilling to show his true feelings, masking his emotional pleasure under a superficial gloss of wit and bitchery.

Jonathan smiled. What fun having both his former workmates under the same roof!

The days passed quickly and serenely with Gloria slowly growing out of her punk style and Henry spending a lot of time "investigating possibilities", as he called it. He was turning into an extremely good organiser, and had trimmed down the staff at the house ("Saving you some pennies, dear!"), held long meetings with Jonathan's accountants ("checking up on how much they've been swindling you out of, darling"), and briefed his employer regularly every day on progress. He'd bought a few new three piece suits from Harrods and looked dapper and smart from the neck down.

Sometimes a drop of blood or two from a squeezed spot appeared on his silk collar, but he would rapidly change to retain his sartorial elegance.

He and Gloria were wary but polite, never too close or in each other's company. Jonathan was surprised – he'd felt that two old co-workers would get on famously. Perhaps the change in scenery needed getting used to. Every now and then he jogged Henry about further developments on the mannequin front, but Henry merely snapped that he was fully occupied with that situation and that Jonathan didn't want an inferior man through rushing him, did he?

So Gloria and Jonathan swam in the luxury pool, sat and talked on the pedestals of the two giant stone horses his father had erected instead of lions at the stairs between house and lawn, walked through the vast estate, and did everything possible to occupy leisure time except visit the stables. They watched old Marilyn Monroe movies on the home video machine, and Jonathan commented how sweet the actress was. Gloria had long worshipped Monroe and this was all the incentive she needed. One afternoon she went in the Rolls to London and returned as a dizzy platinum blonde, her hair bleached further out of punk and curled where necessary to give the desired effect. Her lips were pouting and red, her eyebrows plucked and shaped, her teeth brighter than nature intended. She wore a large, woolly, white cashmere sweater and a pair of old-fashioned light blue denim jeans. Her newly collected contact lenses gave her a mystical, confused, vacant expression except when she fell over furniture or toppled ornaments to the ground.

"What d'you think, lovey?" she asked.

"Well, I much prefer it to the punk look, Gloria," said Jonathan, backing away slightly.

"Let me play Marilyn for you, sweetipie, and sit on your lap and be your little kitten," she whispered in a cooing voice, pouting a well-rehearsed smile that was rather more a grimace.

She wriggled towards him and knocked over the tea table with a crash. Jonathan leapt up to save it and Gloria missed her aim at him and sprawled head first onto the carpet.

"Me lens! I've lost me lens! Help me look for it, love, it cost a fortune."

48

In this position Henry came across them, combing the floor with dampened fingertips for a small plastic shell.

"What *are* you two up to?"

"Ooh – don't move, love. I've lost me contact lens. It's here somewhere."

"Got it!" said Jonathan, with pride, as his hand brushed against the little bubble of miraculous plastic.

"Thank God," said Gloria, resting back on her buttocks and sitting straight on top of a jagged piece of broken bone china which lacerated her Levi's and cut a neat wound into her bottom.

"Ow," she screamed, leaping upwards, hurling Jonathan sideways and sending the contact lens flying from his hand into infinity. Henry screamed with hysterical laughter and Gloria, incensed by a combination of injured pride, eyesight and backside, slapped him across the face in a crack of thunder. The chauffeur, standing behind Henry, almost choked with stifled derision. Henry went purple with fury and stormed out. Jonathan picked himself out of the debris and tried to tidy up the mess of physical and mental cataclysm resulting from Gloria's change in appearance.

She, poor girl, collapsed in floods of tears, so he gave her a comforting cuddle which she accepted with alacrity, smearing lipstick all over him. Passing her hastily to the chauffeur to escort her to her bedroom and instructing him to call the doctor to deal with her injury, Jonathan rushed after Henry, who was packing his bags.

"Either that woman goes or I go," he seethed, lisping venom and bile from between slightly swollen lips.

"I've been physically attacked. Scarred for life. She's not sane. She's a raving lunatic, darling. One moment Johnny Rotten, the next Jayne Mansfield, causing death and destruction wherever she goes!

Check out her passport for a visa to Hiroshima, honey!"

Jonathan soothed and stroked his ruffled employee and after a number of very complimentary remarks plus a rise in salary to two thousand a week, Henry repented and agreed to continue.

"I don't really dislike the girl, sugar. It's just that she's so highly strung."

Jonathan then went to Gloria's room where she was prostrate on her chest, make-up smudged beyond repair, blonde locks hanging in abandon. After some words of sweetness and a compulsory examination of the troubled area, he persuaded her to apologise to Henry, which she did willingly and sincerely, blaming the hysteria of the moment. The doctor arrived with the chauffeur and patched up the wound. As Jonathan sat downstairs with a large Bloody Mary, trying not to look at it while he sipped, Henry told him the good news. He'd found a specialist – a genius – the ideal man for the job. Respected throughout the profession, eulogised in *The Lancet*, praised to the skies by experts everywhere. His practice in South Africa and Britain brought him vast sums of money, so his time would not be cheap, but – if anyone could give life to the mannequin – he surely was the man to do it.

The world of healing and medicine. The staff of life, the serpent of learning. Surgeons, transplants, mechanical organs, kidney machines, artificial lungs, pacemakers. A universe of complexity and dedication. A new sphere of humanity, taking over where St Francis of Assisi had left off. From Darwin to Barnard; if anywhere, there lay the answer.

Dr Anthony Smooth had an extremely impressive suite of offices just off Harley Street. Jonathan and Henry were ushered into a waiting room so deeply piled in carpet that Jonathan wondered whether patients often broke their ankles before audience.

The antiques were worth thousands of pounds; a painting by Salvador Dali hung grandly on the wall with a melting clock dominating the scenario. No tacky *Country Life* or *Harper's* adorned the tables, but rich, leather-bound volumes graced the shelves. The receptionist, who the uniformed doorman introduced them to, was glossy in the extreme and looked perfectly inflated by manual means. Her teeth alone were obviously created from the finest African ivory and her eyes could have been diamonds but were, at the very least, expensive cut glass.

After an acceptable few minutes of waiting she ushered them through a handcarved neo-oak door into the presence. Dr Smooth oozed charm from his golden suntan to the inch of white shirt cuff protruding from his tailored sleeves. He had rather a nasty cough.

"How do you do, Lord Farting?" he said to Henry, as he pumped his arm up and down firmly, "I'm not a skin specialist, I'm afraid, but I'm sure I can do something for you."

"No, no," choked Henry, only just able to speak, "*this* is Lord Farting," which Jonathan wasn't, but Henry decided it was wise and prudent to retain the title for reasons of accessibility.

"I beg your pardon," said Smooth, his radiant blue eyes sparkling with a thin veil of charm, "please take a seat."

They rested on padded velvet cushions and outlined their problem to him. He listened respectfully, his fingertips pressed together in the shape of a manicured pyramid. His brow furrowed every now and again in serious contemplation of the situation and small lines creased his elegant forehead just between the relentlessly brushed touch of white hair above his sideburns. He coughed into a cotton handkerchief.

When Jonathan had finished, Dr Smooth allowed the atmosphere to settle back to the ordered quiet of his surgery and spoke in a deep, soothing, hypnotic voice which would have thrilled a country and western disc jockey with pride.

"You may or may not know of my medical career, Lord Farting, but, in case the latter is true, allow me to precis a brief synopsis. I have perfected the art of transplant in surgery. I can give the heart of a goat to a human being, the penis of an elephant to a dwarf, the sinus of a reptile to a hay fever-suffering housewife. The rejection rate in my operations is minimal. But – even though my skills are – in due modesty – incredible, I have to allow my actions to be motivated by a very strict ethical code.

"Should an animal be killed to invest a human with life? When can you consider a corpse to be legally and morally dead? How far can a mere surgeon go in creating the pulse of existence in a body bereft of soul, denied the breath of survival by some greater and more lasting power?"

He paused to cough for a moment and gazed at the delicate chandelier hanging from his splendid ceiling. His cuticles grew white from the pressure of this emotional moment. A breeze from the open window fluttered the brown paper wrapping of the X-rays of a cancer suspect lying on his desk.

"Given this enormous responsibility," he continued, "I have to rely on the depths of my intuition to guide me in my actions. I have no doubt at all that, given the right assistance, tools, and faith, I could accomplish the goal you so desperately seek. But my art is not to bring life to the hollow shell of man's fickle desires."

His voice grew stern; his gaze more condemning; his skin more creased with effort. He spat some mucus into a tissue.

"I fear I cannot be of use to you in this matter. More – I suggest you should seek professional advice about this obsession which could destroy you, Lord Farting, and your friends." He fixed an analytical stare on Henry, obviously regretting the vaporisation of a much more rewarding problem.

"I know a brilliant psychiatrist who might be of deep assistance to you in your quest. Whether or not he could suggest a permanent solution, I am not qualified to guess. But I would seriously recommend that you visit him as soon as you possibly can and apprise him of the facts in this case."

Dr Anthony Smooth scribbled a few words on a piece of paper and held them out to Jonathan as one might pass a vital organ to a leper. Rising, bowing, and thanking him for his time, Jonathan and Henry felt rather as though they were leaving the presence of the Pope. Jonathan had a crazy desire to exit backwards. He resisted the temptation, knowing such behaviour would only convince Dr Smooth of his total insanity, and the two of them passed out of the luxury into the relative normality of the Rolls without speaking.

"What a fake!" burst out Jonathan, and Henry screamed with laughter.

"You must admit he's got front, honey," he said. "Anyway, there's no harm in paying this other man a visit – if only for reasons of amusement."

Back in the peace of the office, Dr Smooth had picked up his trim-phone and dialled a number.

"Yes, quite crazy – but not dangerous. A number of sessions should see the problem solved. Fascinating preoccupation, though. Never seen one so firmly fixed before. No, of course normally we'd just leave it be. But he's loaded with money – one of the richest men in the world – and he's liable to keep spending until he finds a satisfactory solution. Which could, of course, result in secondary problems for a lot of ordinary people. I think you should see him, if only for the good of society. Not at all, you're very welcome. See you at the club."

Putting down the phone he allowed a series of

racking bursts to explode from his lungs before lighting a cigarette and buzzing for the next patient.

Gloria was up and about again when they got back to Farting Castle, propped delicately against some rich cushions and wincing at every movement. Jonathan had, at Henry's suggestion, bought her another pair of contact lenses from her optician and she trilled with gratitude as she went through the unpleasant ceremony of plopping them onto her eyeballs. Henry went off to some meetings about the estate and Jonathan sat talking to Gloria as the sun streaked through the curtains and flecked the Persian carpet with lines of bright fire.

"God, the dramas that happen! Would you believe that scene yesterday if you read it in a book? Anyway, that's all over now. How did your session with Harley Street go, love?"

"Not too well, I'm afraid. He told me I should go to an analyst."

"Well, there's no harm in that, is there? You pop along and let him know all your little secret lusts and desires and he'll put you straight in no time. Not that I'm criticising your ideas," she added hastily, seeing a steely look creep into Jonathan's eyes, "but there's no harm in a little variety, is there? Now, look, Jon – I need some advice. Do you think in this day and age, a feller minds if a girl's gone and slept about a bit? I mean – take yourself. What would *you* feel if you fell deeply in love with a bird and she told you she'd had it off somewhere else?"

Jonathan had never seriously contemplated this possibility, but he thought he should make himself as agreeable as possible and, since Gloria had returned to her favourite topic, she was obviously feeling better.

"I don't think I'd worry. After all, a lot of boys, these days, experiment around before settling down.

As long as she hadn't been a complete slut I don't feel it would be that important."

"A complete slut! Come off it, Jon, I'm not suggesting I should hang up a red light outside my bedroom – though some of the girls might just as well, the way they go on." She sniggered, and adjusted her breasts in the blouse she was wearing since her official Monroe pullover was showing signs of yesterday's battle and had been sent to the cleaners.

On the excuse of freshening up after the day in London, Jonathan went upstairs and wandered into the main bedroom. The mannequin was lying peacefully on the bed, no complicated virginal queries emanating from her mouth, no disturbed vibrations about love or romance hanging over her head. Beautiful and at rest, her perfectly proportioned face held his gaze fascinated and amazed. He could never fully accept her magical quality. Somehow, every time he saw her she looked different. Now she was calming him, telling him not to worry, that everything would work out all right in the end.

Gloria's common squawks echoed in his head, with their unspoken pressures and hangups, their relentless repressed sexuality. Henry's giggles and umbrage flowed into his mind, tense and nervous, bitchy and hysterical. Dr Anthony Smooth's cough rattled his brain cells and irritated his memory even more than his supercilious and derogatory advice. None of them could know the still waters of his relationship with this strange lady. None of them could ever experience the relaxation that was his.

He left and went back down to the drawing room. As he passed Henry's door he heard a crash of glass and an explosive swear word. Rushing in, he saw the chauffeur picking up a large porcelain horse and raising it above his head.

"What on earth are you doing? Have you gone mad?" asked Jonathan.

"No, dear, it's nothing – don't worry," said Henry, cowering in a far corner of the room, "just a touch of Latin temperament. I was criticising certain aspects of the maintenance of the Rolls and I'm afraid my remarks were taken personally. I'm sorry, dear," he shouted at the chauffeur, "I didn't mean to disturb you."

Casting a macho glare at both of them, the chauffeur stalked out.

"My God, this is ridiculous," said Jonathan. "The house won't be left standing if anything else is broken."

"Nothing serious, honey."

"Well, I don't know. Perhaps we should get rid of him if he's displaying moments of violence. I don't think I like the idea of being driven about by someone who loses his temper so easily."

"No, no, no, darling. It's fine. All my fault. I think I challenge his masculinity! You can't fire someone for being butch, dear. The fabric of society would crumble!"

Since Henry seemed so capable of coping with everyone else, Jonathan shrugged his shoulders and let matters rest. Downstairs, he found the chauffeur talking to Gloria and puffing up the cushions around her to make her more comfortable.

"I think you should get rid of that young man," she said, when he'd left. "I don't feel safe when he's in the room."

"Really? I thought he was taking care of you rather well," said Jonathan.

"*Too* well, love, I think he's got designs on my body. There's a funny look in his eyes when he speaks to me."

Oh dear, thought Jonathan, the complicated hang-ups people create out of their own confusion. Once more, the remembrance of his beloved flooded into his soul and brought peace and quiet and tranquillity.

There was a definite atmosphere in the car as they drove into London the next morning. Lord Farting had acquired one of the few long wheel base Rolls Phantom limousines designed and built by James Young from an earlier Silver Cloud model and it purred along the road with no problem at all, maroon and gold in colour, with warm beige cloth upholstery and deep pile carpet. The chauffeur wore a dark suit and grey cap with Farting insignia blazoned upon the peak. He sat silent in the front compartment. Henry, Gloria, and Jonathan were equally silent in the back; Gloria shifting obviously on her still tender patched backside; Henry pouting and staring out of the window, preoccupied with matters of business; Jonathan wondering why he was submitting to cross-examination by an analyst he neither respected nor required. The clock ticked quietly and the only real sound was Henry playing with – and eventually breaking – the electric cigar lighter in the ashtray on the armrest.

"This car doesn't sound too bad to me, Henry. What do you think is the matter with the engine?"

"Really, dear, can't you tell bad timing when you hear it?" Henry's awareness of bad timing did not run to motor engines, but that was not actually to the point. "And look at the trim here," he said, tugging a piece of perfectly glued leather away from its anchorage. "Not to mention this cigar lighter, which doesn't work."

"You just broke that yourself, fiddling with it."

"Well, if you're going to take *that* kind of attitude, darling, I might as well shut up and go home. Anyway – I said it was all being looked after, and it has been."

He wound down the partition at the touch of a button.

"You've corrected the engine problem, haven't you, dear?" he queried.

A sound like a bark crossed with a burp grunted

from the front seat and Henry hastily raised the partition again.

"So, what's the name of this man and where does he operate from?" asked Jonathan.

"It's a Dr Peter Smooth and he has rooms in Knightsbridge. I suspect he may be a relative."

That seemed a fair conclusion. The chauffeur parked the car in Hans Place, a pretty square next to Harrods, and they walked down Walton Street to a slightly tatty white house with fake Roman pillars and a small statue of Athena in the overgrown garden. Gloria nearly tripped in her stiletto heels on the crazy paving, and stubbed her toe on the steep and irregular steps leading up to the front door. A middle aged lady answered the bell, which had seven tones and played a musical riff Jonathan recognised but couldn't name. She was ruffled and flustered and ushered them into a room as she juggled with pince nez and made them repeat Jonathan's name four times. A few seconds later she returned, dragging her fingers through her unkempt locks, and told them Dr Smooth would see them now, please.

Dr Peter Smooth stood up to welcome them and knocked over a cup of coffee which drowned several files in brown liquid.

"Mrs Patterson, Mrs Patterson, help! A cloth, please, a cloth! I'm terribly sorry, hello, I believe you've met my brother who's kindly referred you to me. He's a brilliant surgeon – quite brilliant – the success of our family. I hope you liked him! I'm sure you did. Everyone does. Anyway, please sit down. Mrs Patterson, Mrs Patterson!"

After mopping up operations had been completed, Dr Smooth suggested that Henry and Gloria might like to wait next door, but Jonathan insisted that he had no secrets from his friends, so the psychiatrist moved them to chairs near the windows and asked Jonathan to explain his problem.

"Well, I don't regard it as a problem," said Jonathan, outlining the situation.

"Aah," said the doctor, meaningfully, wiping his forehead and exhaling deeply. "I can see why my brother suggested you should pop along here. Why don't you lie down on the couch?" He cleared some large medical textbooks off the offending chaise longue and Jonathan stretched out on it, feeling relaxed and rested.

"Yes, my brother could always spot the seeds of psychological disorders at an early stage. Not that I'm saying you're insane, you understand. Over the years many analysts have investigated mental conditions with varying but tolerable results. My brother was always excellent at noticing the signs. When we were small he used to sort out all *my* problems; you know, family dramas and adolescent neuroses. Quite often I would despair of accomplishing anything, especially as he always did so well in school and as his career was always so promising. But he was always there to back me up – the elder brother, reliable, upstanding, glamorous."

He paused and gazed through the window, oblivious of Gloria, blonde and tawdry, nervously shifting in her seat and Henry, fidgeting with his pimples.

"Even now he is the brilliant and successful surgeon, sending me cases, referring titled and wealthy people to my practice. Always referring, always helping. Why – he even got me into the chic Virginia Close Golf Club that only wildly famous executives can join. Almost everything I am I owe to him. How, I sometimes wonder, can I ever repay him?"

Outside the cry of merry shoppers was mingling with the purr of expensive motor engines and the footsteps of happy traffic wardens. The summer air wafted through the lace curtains.

"You think you have a problem, worshipping a mannequin. Imagine how I feel, indebted to my own flesh and blood, looking up to him, reading about him, hearing his praises sung by all manner of voices. People refer to me as Dr Anthony Smooth's brother!"

Jonathan glanced at him. He seemed close to tears, and he certainly didn't look younger than the consultant. What little hair he had left was salt and pepper, orange and grey, wispy and dishevelled and sticking up in spikes and feathers. His face was lined with worry and creased with indecision. He wore hornrimmed spectacles mended on the arms with Sellotape and his shirt collar was frayed. He kept fiddling with his teeth.

Dr Peter Smooth stood up and began to walk backwards and forwards. He was talking nonstop. Jonathan had always thought analysts got their patients to ramble on about their complexes. Dr Smooth seemed to specialise in a revolutionary new style. It was making Jonathan nervous.

"So there we are. Dr Freud says one thing, Pavlov says another, and here we are trapped in the middle of it all without guidance of any cogent kind."

Jonathan wondered whether he'd missed anything of importance and decided he hadn't.

Dr Smooth sat down at his desk. "Well, Lord Farting, I shall have to see you again. Please make another appointment with Mrs Patterson. Mrs Patterson! Mrs Patterson!"

The lady in question rushed in and Dr Smooth stood up to bid his guests farewell, knocking over the anglepoise and tipping the contents of his "in" tray onto the floor.

"Lord Farting will telephone to make a further appointment. Goodbye, goodbye."

Henry insisted they return to the Rolls by way of the men's department in Harrods, where he purchased some more suits, and the beauty counters, where he bought some Bee Pollen Plus extract that Dr Anthony Smooth had recommended by phone for his complexion blemishes. He and Jonathan agreed that Dr Peter Smooth was not nearly as impressive as his brother, but considerably more sincere. Gloria said she thought she'd twisted her ankle and would have to lie down again when they got back to Farting Castle. She had rather liked Dr Smooth. An element of accidental compatibility.

Progress round the elegant halls of Harrods was rather hampered by Gloria's injuries, and they spent an hour limping from marble food halls reeking of salmon and meats to fruit departments fragrant with vitamin C, and perfume emporiums heavy with man-made odours culled from the glands of small mammals. On their way out they passed the computer games section of the store and a shrill voice cried out.

"Henry, darling! Over here, dear! Well, well, what a coincidence! How have you been, honey?"

A Henry clone was standing behind a counter dispensing calculators and electronic video toys. He was neatly dressed in a standard floorwalker suit with a tiny button proclaiming H in green in his lapel.

"Sweetie," shrieked Henry, "you're wearing my badge!"

They howled with mutual lack of amusement and exhanged pleasantries about their social lives.

"How long have you been here?" asked Henry. "Used to be at Selfishes," he explained to his companions.

"Oh, quite some months," said the clone, adjusting a blemish. "It's very interesting. You know I didn't realise the business these games people do. *Creatabot*, they're called. The biggest company in the silicon chip world. *Anything*, dear, *anything* you want they've made."

He waved a white hand over the vast display of digital watches, miniature TV sets and assorted gimmicks. Henry looked at Jonathan. "Are you thinking what I'm thinking, darling?" he asked.

Jonathan wasn't doing much thinking, actually. He

was depressed by the lack of success they'd had and was pessimistic about ever finding a solution.

"Look at this," said the clone, fishing into a drawer in the vicinity of his groin and removing a doll-like figure about two feet tall. "One of our new lines. *Creatagal*. She'll do almost anything a person could want. *Almost*," he repeated, with a snigger.

He placed the figurine on the glass top of the counter, and pressed a button on a little black box. Jerkily, the robot took steps forwards. Another button and she opened her eyes. Two at once and she lifted her arms and nodded her head simultaneously. She was dressed as a maid, in a frilly lace outfit with matching black fishnet stockings. The clone pressed another switch and the doll squeaked a noise.

"What was that again, dear?" asked Henry.

"Master," peeped the homunculus in a mechanical belch, and she turned around like a ballerina.

"Magic, isn't it, darling," squealed the clone. "Every day something new comes along. Never a boring moment. Makes a nice change from the dreary old routine of Selfishes, I'm afraid. Still there, are you, pussy?"

Henry took great pleasure in informing his acquaintance of the alteration in his circumstances and in introducing him to one of the richest men in the world. The clone's eyes grew quite misty with desire and a drool of saliva gathered in the corner of his slighty caked mouth. Noticing this physical deterioration, Henry said his goodbyes and whisked Jonathan away as the clone was desperately searching for suitable small talk to develop the relationship.

"Well, honey, I think that should be our next port of call."

"What do you mean?"

"Creatabot. A couple of notes to the chairman and I'm sure you'll be welcome to do the grand tour of factory, workshops and so on. Think, darling. Scientists, engineers, mechanics – all under one roof. All

62

spending their lives conceiving new ways of simulating reality. Surely your challenge must excite them."

"I hadn't thought of that," said Jonathan, "but it sounds rather automatic. Soul-less. I'm not sure I'd like her to twitch about like that horrid doll."

"No, no – don't examine the practical examples of their work so far. Think of technology. The future will be a blaze of successful experiments in science. Why not pioneer one of the greatest?"

It was a valid point of view. In the car Jonathan allowed his mind to dwell on the prospects and he became quite elated as Henry and Gloria recited and absorbed various filthy stories concerning the person they had just left.

Science. Darwin had been a scientist. Biology had moved in two directions. The medical universe had proved non-cooperative and useless, so why not try the other side? Man could put foot on the moon. Planets could be conquered entirely due to the skills and crafts of scientists, engineers, mechanics. Who could have imagined rockets, airplanes, televisions? And where, he thought to himself, would the world of medicine be today without scanners, X-ray, machines, miniaturisation. Of course, this was the road to the future! He almost hugged Henry in his joy. The silicon chip. There, if anywhere, lay the answer.

Henry had summoned Jonathan into the study. This was a pleasant, open room in light oak with a view out of the front of the house, over the rolling lawns and across the acres of fields and meadows that culminated in a small wood and, just out of sight, the stables. Henry had taken over this library as his office, and mounds of neatly piled paper cluttered tables and shelves. Every day, a young male secretary arrived from town in his compact economy car and, efficiently, typed replies, paid bills, took dictation and insults and rendered unto Caesar the things that were not.

Henry had a series of credit cards in order to charge expenses against all the various international holding companies with a minimum of tax. Even Jonathan's accountants had been impressed by the speed at which Henry – a layman in the religious order of finance – had mastered tax laws, contracts, company business, and corporate investments.

Jonathan had found that the burden of ceaseless requests and demands from his professional advisers had been lifted from his shoulders and slipped gently into Henry's pockets. A born organiser, his friend would have been a magnificent chancellor to an early Roman emperor – quietly by his side, inserting documents under the imperial seal, whispering discreet advice into his ear. For when Henry was firing on all cylinders, his outrageous mannerisms calmed to a studied efficiency. He'd even acquired a studious pair of hornrimmed spectacles which perched on his nose in plain glass splendour, adding a serious note to all proceedings.

Once a day, Henry briefed Jonathan on the runnings of his empire. Where the money was going, who was buying and selling, why such and such was happening and so on.

On these occasions Jonathan drifted off into a day dream, hypnotised by the sudden change from raucous, shrieking extrovert to monotonous, sensible executive. Today Henry was informing his employer about changes on the estate, some hiring and firings he had felt necessary. Jeeves the butler had been remaindered. He was too old, too subservient, too disapproving, too reactionary. Three more rooms were being converted into offices in order to be able to write off extra space against tax. Anyway, existing work areas were insufficient and Henry intended bringing four or five more assistants in from London to help organise things. A telex machine was being installed and a helicopter purchased to facilitate travel during rush hours.

"What about our trip to that computer factory," asked Jonathan, who was bored very quickly by matters of high finance and big business.

"That's in hand. We should be able to go up there within the next couple of days. I'll keep you informed. Now, as to the matter of staff transport . . ."

Jonathan phased out again, his mind wandering along more interesting routes.

Later that day he was strolling around the gardens with Gloria. They sat at the hoofs of one of the stone horses, rampant and designed to be similar to the monstrous gold statues in St Mark's Square in Venice, and allowed the calm Berkshire breeze to cool their faces. Since May, Britain had been experiencing one of its rare heatwaves and the green of the grass and shrubbery gleamed like velvet cushions.

"Can I tell you something, Jon? You won't mind if I swear you to secrecy, will you. You're the only person I could ever say this to; you're special to me, love, you know that, don't you?"

Jonathan smiled a polite reply.

"Well, I've gone and done it! I've made up me mind on the spur of the moment and – pop – off it went, the way of all good things."

She paused, and looked nervously at her friend for his reaction.

"You don't mind, do you? You're not annoyed, or shocked, or anything? I did ask you what you thought. I'd never have done it if I'd thought you'd despise me or look down on me or anything."

After all these months of Gloria's relentless virginity, Jonathan did, in fact, find himself rather taken aback by this news. He managed to suffocate an impulse to giggle and stammered out an assurance of his tolerance and a query as to how, and why, this earth shattering development had taken place.

65

It seemed that, recently, the chauffeur had taken to helping Gloria to her room and had given her a very relaxing and, at first, platonic massage as she lay on her mammaries and eased the pressure on her aching backside. Slowly he had begun stroking the injured area, talking soothingly and gently to it as he did so. His voice had stiffened and hardened as her buttocks had contracted and ebbed under his soft fingertips. She, in turn, aware of the erect vibrations in the air, had discovered, to her astonishment, that her breasts felt as though they were pressed into two little pellets of metal. This unusual sensation strangely titillated her. As a result she began squirming slightly beneath his touch and he had started to continue the massage utilising rather more of his body than originally intended. Suddenly she noticed an even more forceful pressure being inserted on her rear areas and, to her amazement and dismay, found herself uncontrollably excited by this prodding. Moments later Gloria was no longer a virgin and red and white stains had mingled politely on the golden cloth of the guest bedspread.

A slight silence followed Gloria's revelation. A few crows fluttered out of a copse of elm trees and a white rabbit scampered on its way across the sward aiming, doubtless, for Watership Down and the burrows of Fiver, Hazel, and all.

"You sure you don't mind, Jon? It was really nice, actually, love, and we've done it quite a few times since. Of course, I've had to organise some little essential protections. Funny, after all those hangups, it seems silly I ever worried about it. Such a trivial molehill to make a mountain out of."

Jonathan made some polite and enquiring small talk.

"Nothing mental, you understand love. Just good old physical lust. No real close friendship, like you and me've got. Anyway, it's all practice, isn't it? I reckon I'll be a fantastic turnon to Mr Right whenever he decides to come along."

She leered at him in a suggestive and mildly repulsive way, her porcine features wrinkling up and her pudgy chin dimpling naughtily. She was back in the woolly white rollneck and some of her bright lipstick had smudged onto her teeth. Jonathan wondered whether the chauffeur preferred her face up or face down.

Later that evening he was watching television with Henry and caught himself contemplating the thought that both Gloria and the chauffeur appeared to have gone to bed early. Since a commercial break seemed to be stretching itself into the length of a short programme, he mentioned to his old friend and one-time fellow gossip in the Selfishes days that Gloria had finally succumbed to the fever of temptation.

Henry went very still and didn't seem at all amused. Normally, thought Jonathan, he would have hooted with laughter and bitched on for hours about the deficiencies of womanhood. Doubtless all this executive activity was damaging his sense of humour.

"Really, dear? Who to?"

Jonathan told him, expecting an explosion of derision. Henry merely yawned and looked at his watch.

"Time for bed I think, darling."

All work and no play makes Jack a dull boy. Jonathan made a mental note to encourage Henry in a bit of old dissolute behaviour before he became all employee and no fun.

Next day a succession of young men in neat suits arrived at the door and were ushered into the study. At lunchtime in the elegant dining-room Gloria was wearing her dark glasses and seemed to have mixed some purple into the rouge of her makeup. Her lips were totally over the top; so much red had been caked onto them that they looked quite swollen and puffy. Jonathan almost mentioned the fact but decided criticism would be tactless, especially as she seemed to have a bad headache and was very silent. Henry was not teasing her or even looking in her direction. Perhaps he's become a prude in his old age, thought Jonathan.

That afternoon he took the car into the village and was surprised to see a new driver behind the wheel – just hired this morning, he was informed. Henry told him, when he returned to the castle, that the chauffeur's insolence had become too much; that his indiscretions with household guests was unforgiveable and not – as Jonathan seemed to think – at all amusing; and that, anyway, the Rolls was in a disgusting condition and needed a properly trained mechanic to nurture it at all times. The new chauffeur, twenty-two and fair-haired, with an attractive pout to his mouth and a cheeky sense of humour, was an East End lad that Henry had met at a friend's house. He had done two weeks, training at an uncle's garage and knew an engine inside out.

Jonathan privately suspected that he and Henry had been closer friends than officially admitted, but his manager seemed to be running the house well, and his private life was, after all, no affair of Jonathan's.

Gloria kept to her room for a couple of days, blaming a touch of the flu, and when she returned to civilisation no mention was made of her lost lover. To himself, again, Jonathan thought a row had blown up between the two of them that had caused Henry, sympathetic to poor Gloria's feelings, to fire the man who, after all, had always had a terrible temper.

Soon Henry announced that a visit had been set up to the Creatabot factory in Newcastle-upon-Tyne, a quaint little Northern town where the inhabitants drank warm brown beer and spoke their own language. Rooms were booked at the luxury Gosforth Park Hotel and a picnic was packed into an old hamper the cook had discovered in the attic. They would make a holiday of it, stopping on the way to consume chicken sandwiches, hardboiled eggs, slices of buttered turkey breast and chunks of fresh carved ham washed down with pink champagne and followed by strawberies and cream, cheese and French bread, thermos-hot coffee and thimbles of liqueur. Gloria had come to life again and made a special trip to London to become glamourised for the event. She returned as nature girl, her hair light brown and swinging straight to her shoulders, her makeup subtle and delicate. She wore cotton shirts and slacks and her feet were encased in plimsoles. She looked like a Roedean-educated 1950s piglet.

Even in the party atmosphere of the picnic Jonathan noticed a coolness between Henry and Gloria. But, as the day progressed with good food, fine wine and blazing sun, the three became once more happy window dressers with a day off. They spread a huge blanket in a field under a large tree and consumed gourmet cuisine with merriment. Their greatest problem was the trajectory of an occasional fly; their most physical effort the lifting of food to the mouth. Soon they began discussing old times and nostalgic memories, but by tacit agreement the chauffeur was not referred to.

Their suites at the hotel were crammed with bowls of fresh fruit and with silver ice buckets over flowing with champagne bottles. They dined in comfort and even visited the hotel discotheque, a cavern of flashing lights, gaudy costumes, distorting music and slippery floors. Jonathan went to bed slightly tipsy but content and looking forward to the next day.

Creatabot, sufficiently instilled from above with the event's importance due to Henry's diplomacy, was throbbing with excitement and anticipation. Jonathan was quite a celebrity from the still fairly recent news stories about his inheritance, and the company publicist had lined up hundreds of journalists and photographers to cover his grand tour. He was taken round by the public relations man, and after meeting and shaking hands with various identical executives ranging from the managing director downwards, the explanatory journey commenced.

Men in white overalls and coats nodded and illustrated, ladies smiled and chattered as they packed boxes, machines whined and whizzed. The entourage grew larger and larger. Corridors of vinyl, rooms thick with phials bubbling, carpeted offices and cavernous warehouses and, eventually, the hub of it all, the central laboratory.

"Now this, Lord Farting, is Professor Von Soul, our key inventor. He is the man behind our greatest experiments in miniaturisation and in silicon chips. We stole him from the Americans, who stole him from Proleps, the giant German electronics conglomerate."

Professor Von Soul was a wizened dwarf of a man with skin like old leather and oblong silver steel glasses embedded in his nose. He was very busy and not at all interested. His handshake was like rolled wet paper. He went straight back to work after a cursory Germanic grunt.

Henry stepped forward. "Would it be possible for us to discuss matters in greater detail and privacy with the professor?" he asked.

"By all means," answered the PR man, snapping a look of command at the scientist. "You won't tell them any trade secrets, will you, professor?" he smiled.

The scientist looked unamused and preoccupied. Giving some notes to an assistant he sighed with deeprooted exasperation at ignorant celebrities cluttering up the organised cycle of life, and led Henry and Jonathan into a tiny office crammed with computer readouts and financial projections.

"Can I explain how works the process or in vich

vay comes out product or vot is a calculator or something?" asked Von Soul, shuffling papers.

"No," said Henry, definitely. "But can you answer me this? If we gave you an object already made would you be able to install the equipment to make it walk, talk, move, and so on?"

Jonathan was going to add a comment but Henry hushed him for the professor's answer.

"I don't see vy not. Is possible if machine can be adapted to take all parts. Some changes might be necessary but no reason to affect the outside shape too much. Very expensive, though. Is cheaper to start from centre and vork outvards."

He scratched his head and a flake of dandruff floated peacefully onto the floor from his iron grey hair.

"Money's no object," said Henry.

"Would she be human, though?" burst in Jonathan. "I mean, could she be made to breathe, love, feel and so on?"

Henry put his head in his hands and the German looked disturbed.

"Vot? Human? Of course not. You can't make a human. Robots ve can create. Computers ve can create. Machines ve is here for, not humans."

"But, surely, somewhere in your science there must be the ability to transfer every symptom of humanity to another organism," asked Jonathan. "You've already made creatures that look and feel and talk like people – can't you go the whole way and transfer the functions of the brain and the heart to a model?"

Von Soul backed away from him nervously.

"Vot do you think I am? Dr Frankenstein? You are crazy. You need not mechanics, engineers, technicians. You need doctor. You need psychiatrist."

Henry tried a desperate last tack. "Well, is there no one else in your field who could help us? No one

71

who has taken that extra step from machines to creatures?"

"No, no. The thought is barmy. You is mad. Too many bionic television shows you is vatching."

As he grew more nervous his English became more erratic and hysterical. He kept shaking his head and his unkempt locks were fluttering from side to side scattering scurf everywhere.

"Simulation, yes. Very close simulation – no problem. Look like human. Talk, move, think like human, is possible. But *be* human – never! Cut the skin – you have wires, not flesh. Ask questions – you haf print-out answer from central control point. Never can you make person vith soul! Never! I must go, gentlemen. *Auf wiedersehen!*"

He had backed away from them and was out of the door and scampering off like a pink and white ant before they could stop him.

The public relations man came in with an enquiring smile glued to his face. "You seem to have disturbed the professor? Asked him a question he couldn't answer?"

Henry glossed but Jonathan was distraught – so near and yet so far.

"Is there no one else with more modern ideas? Can you think of nobody who would know more about trends and breakthroughs in scientific knowledge?"

"I can assure you, Lord Farting, that Von Soul is the expert in his field. Modern technology acknowledges him as the master. Any university, hospital, publication connected with his work will guarantee you the same. Why? Was your discussion unsatisfactory?"

The door was open and the atmosphere was electric. Dozens of people gaped and wondered what was going on. They'd all seen the professor scuttle away. They could sense the strangeness in the air. Henry grabbed Jonathan's arm and hurried him through the crowd before he said anything else, leaving Gloria to follow with the PR man. Behind them, confusion reigned supreme. But one grubby reporter, a sharp look in his eye, crept away in the direction Professor Von Soul had taken.

Andy Pirraner had never been a popular boy in the Gorbals in Glasgow. Not that there had been anything wrong with the sperm or the egg which had created him. Any expert who had examined said seeds under a microscope would have pronounced them normal in every way. Any obstetrician would have been satisfied with the development of the foetus. His parents were healthy, if ordinary. But he was not much loved. The red hair and freckles of his race had made his pasty yellow skin look even more unhealthy than it actually was. To avoid the relentless bullying of his compatriots he'd developed a tongue like a razor and a vicious ability to destroy reputations with gossip and rumour spread secretly in dark alleyways and seamy corners. Many victims of Andy's underhand assassinations never realised they'd been morally ambushed and robbed by him.

From school to art college he grew cunning, devious, immoral, and evil. These talents made him perfectly fit for a career as investigative reporter on a local evening newspaper. Never popular, he became increasingly respected and sought after by editors who wanted circulation without soiling their own hands in the liquid that brought it. Thus he matured in stature until he reached the dizzy heights of working as a northern journalist on the most unpleasant national Sunday publication. A rat swimming in the sewer of the printing world, Hatchet Andy had finally arrived in a world that deserved him.

By now his hair was flecked with premature white which had turned the primary colour sandy. His prominent wedge of a nose and sparse moustache, frequently stained with drops of stale beer or particles

73

of nicotine, thrust sniffing out in front of him. A ferret, hunting for news, was how he liked to think of himself.

"Pirraner, *Sunday News*," he introduced himself to Professor Von Soul, who had retired irritable and troubled into the staff canteen for a quiet cup of tea to calm his nerves.

"Vot do you vant?"

"What was all that about?" asked Hatchet Andy, joining the learned scientist and pushing half a dozen lumps of sugar into his own tea, slopping most of the contents into the saucer. "Down there, with his Lordship and the fairy. What did they want? Take-over bid or something? Try to engineer a transfer, did they?"

Von Soul had difficulty in understanding him. He was used to the Geordie accent, but a Scots voice – Glaswegian at that – belonging to a reporter is probably the ultimate in contorted vowels and consonants.

"Crazy men. Too many films. Think I can create a human being."

He looked at the rodent opposite. Could he trust this man to lend a sympathetic ear?

"Haf you seen *The Stepford Vives?*"

Andy remembered a rather good cult movie he'd once seen on a trans-Atlantic airplane when going to Washington to cover a story about a Leeds councillor who was having a homosexual affair with a U.S. Congressman.

"That film about the housewives that were robots?" he queried.

"Precisely. That they vant. The vant another Stepford Vife. All House of Lords is crazy, no?"

"No," agreed Andy, his mind whirring. What on earth was going on? His instinct told him there was a story here. His nostrils quivered.

"They wanted a robot? A business deal? Did they

74

try to steal you from Creatabot? Underhand negotiation?"

"No, no, not a robot. A person. A voman. A human being. They haf the body, they vant the soul. Is not possible, I say. Can I advise someone else, they ask me? They think I am no good. But it is them who is no good. They is crazy."

Disturbed by all this illogical behaviour and troubled by the intensity of the emotional vibrations that had emanated from Jonathan, Professor Von Soul stirred his tea with a troubled spoon and contemplated the world of electronics. A piece of dry skin wafted down from his scalp and settled on the surface of his beverage.

By the time Andy Pirraner had got to the public relations man's office the Farting trio had swept off in the Rolls leaving a bemused and prematurely terminated welcoming party behind at the altar. No reason had been given for the early exit, except that Jonathan was not feeling too well. Andy asked a few pertinent questions about motives for the tour, justification for the visit and so on. Then he squeezed into his Volkswagen and beetled back to his digs in Newcastle. Not intending to live for long in this dreadful city, he had acquired rooms in a central boarding house from which he could suck most of the poison out of the area before recycling to grander premises. The dirty, semi-detached, smoke blackened brick house in the centre of town near the station was perfect for his needs. He parked his battered green car outside and let himself in with a scrape and a clink of his nude stripper keyring. Then he poured himself a Scotch in a chipped tooth mug and slumped into the old armchair to think of developments.

Thoughtfully he picked a chunk of torn skin from one of his brown stained fingers. Then, his cuticle bleeding slightly, he stuck it into the dial of his telephone.

"Hello? Tony? I think I'm onto a fucking monster, man. Can I come down and give you the low down?"

It wasn't long before the car was stowed in the station car park and Pirraner, pausing only to soil the ancient enamel of the stalls in the gents' toilet, was on his way to London.

The entrance to the offices of the *Sunday News* just off Fleet Street was impressive and marble, with a staircase ascending regally to higher regions.

Enter those regions, however, and an oppressive atmosphere of destruction assailed one's nostrils. The stench of hypocrisy and panic-sweat mingled with the odours of urinal alcohol and embryonic cancer of the bowels. Damp corduroys and underarm drip-dry nylon shirts clogged the nostrils already inflamed by smoke from cheap cigarettes. Dried phlegm littered the corridors. Anyone expecting the fresh taste of new cut paper or clean printing ink was severely disappointed. Not here the morals of decent press barons or the chivalry of days spent righting wrongs and helping the oppressed. Trails of hypothetical or-dure led soggy from the toilets into the communal offices and past the telex machines which spat everyday news into the kingdom, ignored, for the most part, whilst excrement was dissected and processed, chewed and savoured.

The men and women working in this dark, evil territory were beady browed and foul of complexion. Their breath smelt like expelled anal air. Their fangs were black and dead with plaque and nicotine. When they laughed there was no humour in the sound, a dry cackle of depravity. Here the keepers of the coun-try's morality wallowed in septic tanks, dressed in second or third hand clothes that once belonged to murderers, never washed, polluted forever with the pungent flavour of ear wax. Hate spawned hate. One and all had in common the cunning, sneaky secret eyes that revealed the weaknesses of others in order to cover up the vile, unspeakable habits of their owners.

Andy "Hatchet" Pirraner was perched on a wooden stool in the office of his editor, Tony Schlimer. Wetting his lips with the thick brown coffee from the office machine, he had already outlined the basic facts of the story as he knew it and Schlimer was gleefully rubbing his hands together in anticipation.

"I think we can give you a front page on this one, Andy, if you come up with the goods. *With* a byline, of course. But you'd better make it fast. Someone else might pick up on it at any moment."

Pirraner had concocted a fictional tale loosely anchored on the facts he'd ascertained and the eventual picture of perversion, corruption, and lust he'd painted was only remotely connected with the reality of the situation. But it was a good story. He'd pieced it together on the train from Newcastle over a packet of crisps and a number of whiskys.

"I need some more details and some atmosphere – family snaps and so on. I'll need a good photographer, of course. Think I can bounce it at you by Friday. Gonna trail it on the box?"

He was referring to the commercials Schlimer took on the television promoting the more interesting contents of that week's issue, usually interspersed with a number of female breasts and the odd spurt of blood.

"No, I don't think so. We'll get the lawyers to look at it, of course, but with his kind of money he could get it stopped if we give him time. Let's keep it all under wraps until it hits the stands."

By devious examination of back issues from the files, Pirraner had found out Henry and Gloria's names and had acquired their addresses and phone numbers from contacts at Selfishes. Aiming at the weakest spot first, he arrived on the doorstep of a tiny semi-detached house in Richmond-on-Thames.

"I believe you have a daughter called Gloria? We're doing an update on that story about the lad she was working with at Selfishes. Yes, I know she's moved from there. Could I come in for a moment?"

He leered an ingratiating sneer with as much charm as a cobra about to strike and pushed his way down the narrow corridor smelling of cabbage to the room at the back.

Any knowledgeable citizen would have slammed the door in his face, especially on seeing he was accompanied by a burly photographer with bag and tripod, but Pirraner was thoroughly professional at getting through blocked entrances and would probably have acquired access somehow anyway. Gloria's family was not knowledgeable. Father was plump and jolly and worked as a bus conductor. Mother was plump and jolly and worked as a cleaner and a housewife and mother to a brood of plump, jolly children of which Gloria was the oldest. Gathered nervously around the television they looked like the little pigs greeting the wolf who threatened to huff and puff and blow their house down.

Pirraner managed to get a number of happy family snaps of them all clustered together smiling nervously, pink and beaming like sausages freshly unwrapped. He also managed to get the phone number of Farting Castle, where Gloria was staying at the moment, dear, and the exact address of same. The other information he wanted was obviously not known by the family, with whom Gloria was an occasional correspondent and not the typical dutiful daughter she should have been. Still, enough was enough. He jotted down numbers and names of friends, details of past boyfriends, interests, hobbies, and favoured colours – all the trivia of childhood that could be refined down to poison in due course. Bidding farewell with a flash of his fingers he jumped back into his hired automatic Ford Granada and, bundling the photographer into the passenger seat, jammed his aromatic foot onto the accelerator and shot off in the direction of Berkshire like a vulture honing in on the rotting corpse of a gold prospector.

THE BOOK
OF FAITH

THE BOOK
OF FAITH

It had been building up inside Jonathan for some time, this feeling that the quest was insane and insoluble. He sat in the bedroom, gazing at the mannequin, filled with sadness and despair. Henry felt sorry for him and almost regretted having encouraged the lunacy. However, Jonathan was obviously no businessman and without this preoccupation he would never have organised his fortunes under Henry's tutelage. By now Henry was officially managing director of the holding company, Farting International, and all of the smaller firms around the world. He also managed the estate and controlled everything except the stables, still functioning by themselves and the object of difficult, lengthy trust examination.

Jonathan sighed deeply and stared out of the window. He had tried everything – all the great minds in all the possible areas – and the answer had been the same. Was he crazy? Was he obsessed by this task of breathing life into the shell of something he already communicated with so deeply? Perhaps it was true – only God could give life and take it away. As those words crossed his mind a deep echo came from the mannequin, a silent message carried on the wings of angels. "Believe!"

He sat back, quite shocked. But, no, there it was again. "Believe!"

Jonathan had never really given much time to

religion. Standard school and university guidance had bored him, and most of his fellows, to tears. Whether or not there was a deity was a question that neither interested nor disturbed him. But this was an incredible feeling. He remembered the expression "born again". He was buzzing, dizzy, confused, impressed. For a moment, he lost the use of his senses. He felt as though an evangelist had touched him on the shoulder. Quickly, he looked over at the mannequin. A halo of sunshine beamed through the window and threw a golden circle of light around her head, making her look holy, unworldly, possessed. Gently but definitely her lips moved as her beautiful eyes held his in a living gaze of strength and power.

"Believe!"

Jonathan shot to his feet and rushed down the corridor shouting for Henry who emerged from his study with an expression of disturbed concentration.

"Yes?"

Jonathan burst out words of Jesus and faith and miracles. Henry, obviously convinced his employer had at last cracked, took him by the hand and guided him to an armchair, made him be quiet, concocted a rapid and lethal Bloody Mary and then sat down and asked him to explain his ravings.

"We must find a holy man, someone with communion to God. You've got to track one down. Not a phony or a fake. A real, genuine contact to the Lord."

He paused, and a vision sprouted into his mind. He leapt out of the chair and shook Henry by the shoulders, spilling his drink everywhere.

"The Pope! The Pope! We must get her to the Pope!"

Fortunately Henry had a large quantity of sleeping pills to hand and, giving Jonathan five "to calm you down, dear," he put him to bed with soothing expressions of assurance and optimism. At least this was better than the suicidal mood that had dominated since Professor Von Soul and Creatabot. But it was by no stretch of the imagination a healthy development. Religious mania Henry could live without. And, of all the lunacies, the pervading power of belief most drained the coffers.

Accordingly, the next day Henry summoned Jonathan to his office and sat him down in front of him. He demanded a power of attorney over all the financial dealings of the empire. He explained that, whilst he was quite prepared to go along with Jonathan's visitation and would always try to help achieve the goal they both had, there was a chance some charlatan might sneak into Jonathan's confidence and burrow funds out of their rightful repose.

"I haven't done badly for you so far, have I? You're making money and living comfortably, and I'm trying all I can to solve the difficult ambition in your life. But I have to have some kind of security if you want me to dedicate myself entirely to the Farting empire."

Jonathan was content to give him all he wanted, so Henry got the power of attorney, plus another substantial rise in salary, and a hefty chunk of shares.

Although his complexion was still stucco and usually covered in a film of bee pollen grease, Henry had cut his hair and now, on every level, appeared the complete executive type, neat and smart. His manner had matured and he was nothing like the outrageous but amusing figure that had draped fabrics and pins around the windows of Selfishes department store. He could even bend down, kneel, squat or stoop without crushing his essentials in a lethal crease of trouser material. The subtle influences of lawyers and accountants had curbed his youthful excesses and irresponsibilities. He'd become fascinated by the abilities he'd never known he'd possessed. And the men he was working with, relieved not to have to deal too much with the erratic young son of the family, found Henry an excellent pupil and tolerable master.

"Right, then, dear," he said (some old habits died hard), "the Pope it is. Leave it to me. I've got a few contacts here and there. I'm sure we can organise an audience before long."

Jonathan breathed a sigh of relief. The ultimate power source. The creator. If anywhere, there lay the answer.

Villages in Berkshire, much like villages anywhere in Britain, usually sport at least one quaint old English pub. This is the centre of gossip in the community. Here residents gather to imbibe vast quantities of liquid and burp scandal and rumour into the pungent air. Leaning on the bar, propping up the walls, sprawled in chairs and on wooden benches, aiming blunt darts at a pockmarked board or fiddling with some electronic game or other, the civilised citizens of Great Britain raise to a new level of triviality the superficial conversation learnt at school, at work, and at home.

Andy Pirraner was not in the Blacksmith's Anvil for this reason. He was there to provoke further details about his chosen victim out of the local inhabitants. Settling his photographer, minus cameras, in an anonymous corner of the public bar, he elbowed his way through a perspiring mass of labourers and school teachers until he reached the barman who was pumping pressurised gas and acid out of the cellar into a customer's stomach by route of a glass pot.

"Two pints of bitter, please."

"Long way from home, mate?"

Being a highly intelligent observer of the social scene, the barman prided himself on his uncanny ability to track down the source of an accent.

"Yes, Scotland. You from round here, Jock?"

"Born and bred, mate, born and bred."

Some minutes of froth later, Pirraner managed to twist the topic round to big houses and estates and,

86

as tended to happen in the area, Farting Castle soon reared its head in a natural fashion.

"Very strange, that new boy. Lot of funny ideas. See 'im over there?"

The barman gesticulated at a good-looking Italian youth sitting alone at the corner of the bar.

"Used to be chauffeur up there at the 'ouse. Not any more, though. Dirty work at the crossroads, if you ask me!"

Summoned to provide further liquid to a haunted looking body builder in a torn T-shirt, he made his apologies, took his money and moved off. Andy Pirraner swam over to the table and returned to the counter accidentally bumping into the chauffeur. Amongst profuse apologies a conversation was started. The anonymous corner soon sat three.

After half an hour of probing questions Andy sent the photographer off to harvest further buckets of hop swill and turned to the chauffeur.

"Look, Jock, this could be very big news. I reckon I could get a hefty sum of money for your memoirs. I'd write the story, of course, for half the cash. OK?"

A few moments of negotiating, wrangling, bargaining and deal striking got the financial arrangements agreed. Andy then left the table and went to the phone.

"Not the angle I thought at all, Tony. Much better. Much, much better. Believe me. I think we should pay this bloke for an exclusive. No, I've tried that. He knows what he's got. If we try to go it alone he'll slip it over to *People's World*." That was another weekly news magazine – the deadly rival of the *Sunday News*. "Trust me, Tone. It'll be worth every penny. OK. I'll bring him in. But I don't think we'll be ready to go until next week. This one's really worth waiting for. Fucking monster, Tone. Trust me."

So it was that the rustic quiet of a country English pub, nestling in the folds of Berkshire, became the

Machiavellian birthplace of yet another juicy *Sunday News* exclusive.

Henry, inspired by his rapid wealth growth, was phoning and visiting Catholic names of great importance. A cardinal had accepted a most generous donation to his pet charity. The monk headmaster of a well-known Catholic public school for boys had been overwhelmed by a massive gift to the impoverished chapel fund. The publisher of a successful Catholic weekly newspaper had been excited by his normally staid advertising manager who had rushed into his office with dramatic news about a special supplement in the next fifteen issues. And, as all things must pass, Jonathan got his meeting with the Pope. In fact, a charming letter from Monseignor Rossetti, on Vatican stationery with the light blue watermark of St Peter's, arrived at Farting Castle, postmarked Wimbledon, granting an audience for Jonathan, Henry and Gloria, on Monday next, just over a week away.

They decided to go to Rome some days early and take the opportunity of seeing the pagan sights in the Holy City. Jonathan, however, could not be dissuaded from his desire to take the mannequin with them. Accordingly she was dressed up as lifelike as possible and bundled into the back of the Rolls. At the airport they were given four boarding passes, since Henry had cleared, at top level, the transportation of this art treasure in one of the seats in the first class compartment. Escorting her through customs and immigration caused a number of raised eyebrows and much stifled giggling and comments. Not quite enough planning had gone into the mobility situation, and two young men carrying a bizarre figure through the airport crowds drew intense interest. Every now and then her outstretched and dangling hand would snag a lady's skirt or a child's overcoat. Some travellers jumped on turning round to see a pair of feet approaching horizontally. But the four of them were soon on their way to Rome and, eventually, ensconced in the finest suite in the Grand Hotel on the Piazza della Repubblica. When Andy Pirraner and his burly photographer arrived at Farting Castle uninvited for his acerbic questions and furtive snaps, he found the birds had flown. As a result, stock pics had to be dragged from the files to accompany the front page exposé run with massive banner headlines in that Sunday's *News*.

Graphically and colourfully, the chauffeur told of demeaning duties, of his master's obsession with a window display model, of kinky orgies involving an out-of-work female shop assistant (whose family, pictured, cried of "outrage"), of perversions suggested to him and rebuffed at the very top of the Farting organisation. But the keystone of his story, this extraordinary quest to breathe life into a stockroom dummy, captivated the imagination of millions of added *News* readers. Extra presses were laid on, overtime paid to satisfied employees, vans refilled with petrol and drivers summoned back from relaxing at home. Circulation leapt upwards, more than justifying the six figure sum paid to the source by Andy Pirraner on behalf of his employers.

Several of those copies arrived in the hands of the Vatican staff based in Wimbledon and it didn't take long before the exclusive phone lines between London and Rome were buzzing with hysterical Latin.

That summer was glorious in Rome. They rode the horse-drawn carriage around the Colosseum and Circus Maximus. They peered in awe at the remnants of the Forum, mighty stone pillars shooting upwards. They wandered the cobbled streets and ate pasta and porcini in the restaurants of the Piazza Navona. They gazed at the Tiber and swept up and down on the Big Dipper at the amusement park in Luna Park, Eur.

Jonathan's heart was filled to bursting. The beauty

of the city and the comforting heat of the sun combined with the peace in his soul, anticipating a final, wonderful consummation for his passions.

On Sunday they went in a hired Mercedes to the beaches at Ostia – miles of clean black sand baked hot under a blue sky. Henry drove, relaxing at last in shorts and a T-shirt, howling comments about the butch Italian lads cruising the promenade. They had lunch in the restaurant on the seafront and consumed fresh shrimps and fish caught moments before and rushed flapping to the table.

It had been agreed that Gloria would be replaced at the audience by the mannequin, who, wrapped in cloaks, would be wheeled there in a chair they had bought for the occasion. The situation would be explained to the holy father who would surely understand and grant the extreme benefits of his faith to the dummy.

They returned elated from a day of sunbathing and swimming. There was an urgent message for Henry to call his personal assistant at home in London. Battling with the phones in the Grand Hotel, Henry found an acid ache in the pit of his stomach. Something was wrong, he could sense it in the atmosphere. It took some minutes to get any kind of connection to Britain, and he lay on the magnificent gilded bed and contemplated the ceiling, obviously painted by Michelangelo, of the fabulous suite they occupied. Jonathan, oblivious, stood on the balcony looking at the fountain bubbling in the square, a giant construction of white marble figures. It was baking hot. Small, grubby urchins with bare limbs and beautiful brown eyes with lashes longer than any artificial fibre stole wallets from fat tourists with sunglasses. Cars shot like dodgems around the piazza, hands jammed on horns, a cacophony of noise and speed. Gloria was removing clothes and lotion from her pink body in the vast bathroom.

Henry put the phone down consumed by a combination of terror and fury. For a moment he lay panting on the large white pillows, gasping like a beached dolphin. Then he called Jonathan and outlined the story in all its gruesome detail. Strangely, because most of the truly horrendous passages referred more to Henry and Gloria than to Jonathan, his employer seemed less disturbed than he should have been. Only a filthy innuendo about his relationship with the mannequin brought a flush to his cheeks. He shrugged his shoulders.

"Well, there's no use crying over spilt milk. If that's what they say, there's nothing we can do about it. We know the truth – who cares what they think?"

Such a stoic attitude was not striking any chords with Henry, who grabbed the phone and spat another number at the mouthpiece to the terror of the inoffensive Italian operator.

"There's a lot we can do, dear. Sue the fucking arse off them, for a start, darling. Christ, imagine what my parents will think?"

Jonathan had never visualised Henry as having parents, but he supposed they did exist, and fell silent. Gloria came in and was briefed with the sordid facts. She turned pale, and on hearing about her family's photo and comments, rushed back into the bathroom and locked the door. Henry shot questions at their lawyer, got the number of a top criminal specialist in libel, instructed immediate communication and slammed the phone down again.

"This really is too bad, dear. God knows how it will affect your investments."

"Not at all, I should think," replied Jonathan. "I shouldn't imagine money is very easily offended."

"That dirty little shit," spat Henry. "How dare he tell those lies to the muck rag? Evil turd. Vile creep."

Jonathan left the room, intimidated by this explosion of invective. He felt sorry for Henry and Gloria, understood their hysteria, but, after all, if they had played with fire they could expect the odd burnt finger. Henry had told many more outrageous tales – surely he had anticipated trouble at some point or another in his rebellious life. Poor Gloria was in a slightly different situation. The *Sunday News* had portrayed her as a flirtatious vamp, eager for intercourse and greedy for male flesh, which was really far from the truth. Even so, lust was no great sin these days.

As far as Jonathan was concerned, the story was basically true, and he wasn't ashamed of it. He had indeed fallen in love with a shop dummy and was indeed trying to bring life to it. He didn't care who knew it. Eccentric, strange, unusual perhaps. But hardly immoral, evil or wrong.

Henry caught up with him some time later in the bar, drinking his Bloody Mary with a thoughtful expression as attentive waiters tended to his every need and hovered like dragonflies in brocade and gold. The Grand Hotel has very fine glassware, with the CIGA arms and insignia cut beautifully into its fragile surface. Jonathan wiped several of these antique ornaments from the table when Henry told him of the call from Father Rossetti cancelling the audience the next day. The Pope, he had been told, was overbooked and indisposed. Many apologies had been made. No, there was no chance of another date being fixed just yet.

"They don't want a pervert meeting the Pope, dear – it's as simple as that. You've been labelled as a lunatic, and nobody wants a lunatic loose in the halls of the Vatican. What's more, we can't sue the bloody paper. There's no real case for libel. It was very well phrased – hinting all but confirming nothing. Anyway, that fucking chauffeur signed an indemnity for them. But I'll get even with them. I'll beat them yet."

His voice shrilled with hysteria. Jonathan sat quiet, in the depths of despair.

They are used to temperament in the Grand Hotel. Onassis has had tantrums there. Artistic Italian film directors have rowed with boys before being murdered in shrubbery. Lady stars have hurled crystal cigarette lighters across the dining room. Politely raising their eyebrows, the well-trained staff ignore where possible and exit when not. It's generally an area of calm, the Grand Hotel. The twentieth century shrieks past it in a howl of motors and brakes, but the arches of the Grand driveway shelter peace and quiet. The tall reception area echoes the tiptoed footsteps of the concierge and the whisper of the cashier. The rustle of million lire banknotes wafts down the corridors like a gently cleared throat. Swallow a drink in the small but chic bar behind the porter's desk and you will be served with poise and elegance. A sensitive soul would find it offensive to cough.

Not Henry. He ranted and raged and squealed. Jonathan's show of emotion had been contained in the dramatic sweep of available glassware. Now he was brooding. And, as he smouldered, the remembrance of his quest and its message returned to him.

Henry was all for leaving this dreadful city as soon as possible and getting back to London where he could rip that fucking journalist to shreds, dear, but Jonathan would have none of it. His composure revived, he insisted that they must anyway go to the Vatican, invited or not. To Henry was given the task of how and when.

Henry did not find it easy to concentrate on the mission in hand. His head was a turmoil of insult and injury. They purchased the *Sunday News* at the bookstand by the station, where English papers arrived erratically every day or so, and the direct confrontation caused another paroxysm of hatred. Gloria was speechless and numb, like a slab of uncooked bacon. Jonathan tried a few phrases of consolation, but the poor girl, branded a slut and a whore so recently after losing her virginity, was in a state of shock and took more kindly to being inserted into bed like a leather tongue into a shoe and fed on delicacies and wines until she was maudlin drunk and finally asleep.

The Pope held general audiences for the masses every Wednesday when – after celebrating the service – he mingled with the crowd in St Peter's and touched the fortunate with a blessed finger. The secret was – Henry learnt – to get there very early and thus be in the front. This way you were almost certain to make holy contact.

They rose before it was light and wrapped the mannequin in most of Gloria's wardrobe. Indeed, they were there before anyone else, and, having ascertained the exact route the Pontiff took, claimed a position and held on to it all day. Slowly the crowds assembled until it was time for evening prayer. The sun was going down and the great square in front of the cathedral was a mass of pilgrims and shadows. The statues of the saints on the columns high above peered down like old headmasters. Inside the mighty church the tiny altars glowed and twinkled and the dome loomed serene over their heads. The beautiful pietà was now safe and reinstalled behind a solid glass shield, from whence the Madonna cuddled her child and emanated goodness. Then the Bishop of Rome appeared and mass was said. The atmosphere of hushed and murmured responses, with his strong voice exhorting the faithful, and the pure vibration of belief, was overwhelming. The Pontiff himself looked like a tall, giant baby wrapped in decorative swaddling clothes topped by a huge crown. Jonathan held his breath. They had attracted little attention. Everyone assumed they were with a very sick old lady. Now the moment had come. The Pope moved forward, splendid in purple and white, regal and stiff, surrounded by scarlet cardinals, touching hands, muttering a blessing. He flowed in their direction, coming closer and closer.

Jonathan held his breath. The Italians around him were jostling and pushing like the first day sale crowd at Selfishes. A fat woman next to him looked as though her arms had been squeezed out of a tooth-paste tube. A swarthy man smelt of garlic and pasta. A midget elbowed him in the buttocks and jammed his chin between him and Henry. Then – as the Pope was there – a great jerk of pressure tipped Jonathan into the handles of the wheelchair and the manne-quin flew out, shedding her clothes as she went, clattering naked and obscene at the very feet of his holiness.

Secret Service agents leapt forward, guns at the ready, aimed, prepared to fire, all pointing at the poor dummy, sprawled on the floor of St Peter's. A massive intake of breath could be heard. The Pope – who had startled slightly – regained his composure in a second, took in the entire situation, compre-hended all and, in a graceful motion, touched Jona-than on the forehead with a gesture of compassion. Then he turned, looked from the boy to the dummy and back again and knelt for a brief moment on the cold marble floor of the cathedral, brushing his finger against the face before moving on as if nothing had happened.

Jonathan stood still, amidst a sea of stifled giggles and embarrassment. Voices in Italian queried what had happened, asked questions in hushed voices. Others, equally stifled, explained. Henry was pinned to the spot in horror.

Jonathan had felt strength, understanding, grace, power. He had sensed the charisma of the man and the intelligence. No way did he feel put down, hu-miliated or despised. The Pope's touch had warmed him with love, and his eyes had told Jonathan many things. But the end result was still the same. The mannequin lay on the floor, lifeless. Henry, assisted by affronted and offended priests, was scrambling to push her back into the chair and stuffing the ma-terials on top of her so she looked like a naked lady sitting in a bubble bath of coloured cloths.

He had believed. At that moment, despite the in-dignity of the accident and the terrible rush of blood to his cheeks, he had wiped out all other senses and forced himself into total belief. And he knew without any doubt that the holy father was a good man, a great man with fine intentions and very little doubt about purpose and reason and existence.

But the dummy was still a shop window model. She didn't breathe or move or live. God had failed him. The ultimate power had not been able to accom-plish the impossible. Now there was nowhere else to try.

THE BOOK
OF CHARITY

THE BOOK
OF CHARITY

Italian stringers had cabled the story to Britain and
Andy Pirraner made sure it was the foundation stone
for a marvellous front page follow-on that next week-
end. But Tony Schlimer, always fingering the pulse
of the nation, well aware of the hypocrisy rampant
in his readers who liked to see pictures of donkeys
penetrating schoolgirls with captions howling "WE
MUST STOP THIS TRADE IN FILTH," had spotted an
overwhelming trend of support in the letters the
Sunday News was getting. Sympathy for the poor
young Lord who was so obsessed by his bizarre
quest. Perhaps they saw a kindred spirit as they lay
in their semi-detached beds and reviewed their
empty lives, surrounded by women they didn't like
or men they despised, children they had never
wanted and whose youth they resented, friends they
felt were enemies and jobs that bored them stiff. The
strange fantasy in Jonathan's mind might have found
a twin spark in the dull brains of the *News* subscribers. These leaden lumps of cells, paralysed by drink
and poison, deadened by misuse and consumption
of trivia, lay like dumplings in the heads of millions
of readers without stirring from one day to the next.
The diet of sensationalism had ceased to titillate. A
surfeit of gore and sex had jaded the palate. Unres-
ponsive to the most colourful "vicar rapes grocer"
stories, hypnotised by "transvestite headmaster re-
veals all" exclusives, numbed by "team of house-

wives in tupperware orgy" tales – the one electric charge which made the puddings tremble in the craniums might have been this weird angle of a young boy who had everything, yet yearned for the impossible. And, despite the definitely malicious slant of Pirraner's piece, the public had responded in droves, with thousands of illiterate letters on lined paper, misspelt and blotted with biro ink stains, addressed incorrectly and stamped at an angle, taking Jonathan's side.

As a result, the next week's issue was more poignant and sad than critical and abusive. Andy Pirraner was not at all pleased by this subbing of his original text. He had, if anything, increased the suspicions of sexual innuendo and perversion. A flaming row in Schlimer's office almost resulted in Andy's resignation. He stormed out reeking of self-righteousness and artistic integrity. The editor had not, of course, revealed his reasons for the change in direction. He liked it to appear that he could anticipate a public reaction rather than follow one. Pirraner spat and snarled like a pregnant leopard being robbed of its young but remembered his deal with the chauffeur and collected the cash for the sequel piece without handing in his notice.

Farting Castle too had suffered the benefits of public reaction. The phone was ringing constantly and extra secretarial help had to be hired. After a visit to Richmond Gloria had returned in a more mellow state. Her family, confronted by totally fictional quotes themselves, had been quite willing not to believe the facts concerning their daughter. Indeed, their fame in the area had been welcomed as sympathy flowed from neighbours, free food and drinks were offered and friends rallied in support. The house, when Gloria arrived, had been like Animal Farm with the snuffling and bleating of the sheep, goats, and cows consoling the poor, mistreated pigs.

It was in the mutual interest to keep the wolves from the door.

Henry had been a pillow of strength for Gloria, too. Hurled together in adversity, he had provided an understanding shoulder to cry on, and, now their attitude to the chauffeur was similar, they discovered how much they each had in common. Jonathan had been surprised that, when they had returned to Berkshire, Henry had not pursued a policy of savaging the press but had, instead, locked himself up with financial advisers and spent hours with stockbrokers and accountants rather than with lawyers and hit men. Gloria had rushed to London and changed her appearance dramatically. No longer "country girl," she was now close cropped and boyish, wearing tailored suits and shirts, with no makeup at all. Her face in this new, severe, neo-Lesbian guise was like a naked spoon. She was not an attractive sight. But, under present circumstances, that was fine.

Jonathan himself, saddened beyond measure, had been cheered by the flood of mail to the castle. The occasional lunatic missive, signed "Der Fuhrer" or some other extraordinary pseudonym and obviously penned with a hypodermic dipped in acid, caused the slight twinge of biliousness intended, but the general tone was so kind, so helpful, so sympathetic that his troubled heart was salved.

And visitors arrived at the gates in great number. An entire security firm worked twenty-four hours a day to keep them away. Even so, some appointments were granted and whilst Henry beavered away behind closed doors with the business matters of state, Jonathan allowed an assortment of representatives from various sects, cults, and occupations to spread their wares in front of him and display their assurances that they could achieve what everyone else had failed to accomplish.

Gloria often sat in on these auditions although Henry was nearly always otherwise occupied.

Madame Lisa, the head of the British Oracle Tarot Occult Mediums Society (BOTOMS), had been contacted by a number of psychic sympathisers and turned up as the representative for all forms of legitimate crystal ball gazing, card reading, palmist, seance, and clairvoyant organisations. She possessed prestigious recommendations, being a Spanish-looking lady of forty-three, or forty-four, with polished black hair and very white teeth. Her lipstick had been baked on. She had an attitude of authority and immediately told both of them their fortunes, wonderfully accurate but woefully general. Jonathan had not previously realised how similar the ambitions and self-conceptions of most people were. She examined their hands; spread cards depicting hanging men, and skeletons with shovels, around the table; hypnotised them with her relentless drone of good will and predictions. She smelt strongly of a musky perfume and Jonathan could see beads of sweat around the base of the hairs on her scalp. She fiddled a lot with a gold charm necklace and explained the workings of the occult in detail. Seances were strongly advised but Jonathan would have none of that and balked at wasting time sitting around a table or pushing wooden boards at letters. She produced mounds of evidence justifying the presence of spirits and poltergeists, waffled on about levitation and ectoplasm. Her round green eyes shone with the insincerity of mystic belief as she told the clichés and platitudes of her art.

"You have been unhappy but this will pass. Much money is on the way, believe me, and love will be accomplished. Follow your instincts, not your thoughts."

Gloria was mesmerised by all this and swayed to and fro under the spell of such basic English and such familiar word patterns like a snake with a charmer. Jonathan was fascinated by the effect and the skill behind it. Without doubt Madam Lisa had perfected her abilities, but none of it was getting him anywhere and most of it seemed aimed at acquiring gifts or donations for the various societies she represented. He tolerated her presence until she started asking for the possessions of loved ones to hold and then decided he'd had enough and got rid of her.

They'd borrowed some of Henry's more efficient staff to process the stream of charitable applicants who vowed they had a solution yet were in reality after sums of money. For a while, Farting Castle became a backdrop for a steady stream of eccentric and genuine believers in some life-style or other.

Master Syun Singh was the guru of the largest Indian meditation society. Respectable and honest enough not to be classed with the Scientologists or the Moonies and thus labelled (or libelled) as a crank sect of phonies, they were not so large and intimidating as the Mormons or the Jehovah's Witnesses. That was how the intelligent young man on the phone had described the Singhis to Jonathan, and, whilst not prepared to burrow through all the myriad beliefs available at the drop of a religious hat, Jonathan felt some kind of Eastern faith might be worth investigating.

Nobody could have faulted the venerable aspect of the Master who arrived at Farting Castle in a small rental car driven by one of his disciples. He was not, apparently, out to get vast riches from the Farting coffers nor even to convert the Farting household to the Singh belief, whatever that was. He was well dressed in Indian fashion with a holiness about him and an astonishingly pleasing sense of humour. Jonathan liked him immediately and gave him tea with Gloria on the front lawn. The cucumber sandwiches and silver service went down terribly well. Syun Singh seemed rooted in his belief, which encompassed various theories of reincarnation, metempsychosis and palingenesis, but felt it unlikely that any of his relatives or dearest friends had returned to live as a cucumber, and so ate with a ferocious appetite. He listened to Jonathan's explanation of the situation whilst chewing and sipping, and bowed his head gravely. He was in his sixties and his grey hair swung about his neck, catching every now and then on the thin string of sandlewood beads that were his only decoration. When he spoke, there was a mere trace of Indian accent.

"I wouldn't try to fool you. I don't regard there as being any hope of finding your desire. Only of changing it. Your love for this mannequin seems to me symptomatic of a longing for peace and one-ness. You look at her and see the basics of existence without the aggravations of life. Many people feel this and express it in different ways. I truly believe the only way to marry with the object of your love is to bury yourself deep inside your soul, to examine your essence, to meditate in depth over a period of time. That way you will find peace within the universe, within yourself, and you will manage to do without the object you seek."

His soothing words were not patronising and Jonathan could see Gloria was impressed by the good sense of it all, but the guru was not providing a solution, only an escape route. After a long discussion which he generally enjoyed but with which he entirely disagreed, he bade the holy man goodbye and waved farewell as he zoomed into the empty beyond in his hired Avis.

"Don't you think he made sense, Jon, love? I mean, you've tried everything and it hasn't worked. Why not think of something else?"

Jonathan went to his bedroom and lay down, shuffling through the huge pile of mail opened and examined by one of his assistants.

"Dear Sir, I couldn't help but feel you might be interested in our ecological approach to life. We believe that we are what we eat, that diet is an all important ingredient in our search for peace within ourselves. Nature and not manmade chemicals can bring health and happiness to our poor polluted bodies. Perhaps a short interview with the leader of our group. . ."

"My dear Lord Farting, A close study of your birth chart and the positions of the planets during your conception might be the answer to your problem. It is not generally known that astrological equations can guide mankind down all sorts of paths and assist us in our otherwise leaderless wanderings. . ."

"Sir, I am a necromancer. In days gone by I would have been burnt as a witch, but now I'm allowed to practise my science in peace. I can assure you that by conjuring up the mystic spirits of the dead you will discover the key to the locked door ahead of you. . ."

"Jonathan, I know what you're going through. As a believer in UFOs (Unidentified Flying Objects), I, too, am scoffed at and categorised as a loony. But there is more than meets the eye, and the government agencies attempting to cover up the truth 'for our own good' will one day realise. . ."

So many routes, so many people as lost and as lonely as he was, all offering advice of a guaranteed nature, all quite sure that they had fortunately discovered the purpose and secret of life. Jonathan drifted into a deep sleep and once again dreamed. He rarely remembered his dreams. This night he was violently spinning in the middle of a giant circus big top. All around him were clowns, acrobats, lion tamers, jugglers. He knew them all – there was Syun Singh balancing on a tightrope with a smile on his face. Gloria was training baby seals to bounce balls on their noses. The audience cheered as Madame Lisa dived into a pool of burning liquid. The Smooth brothers were somersaulting around as clowns. But Jonathan was worried. Nowhere could he see the mannequin. He stopped dancing and ran around looking desperately. She must be here somewhere. Henry was cracking a whip at some horses and Mr Gross was riding an elephant. He was panicking. Still no mannequin. Sweat poured from his brow. In his sleep he tossed and turned, drenching the bed in a fever of perspiration, knocking piles of letters onto the floor. Where? Where? He felt himself falling. Darkness was pulling over him, spirited up by the necromancer. The figures grew shady, remote. Slowly they stopped moving, all watching him. Silence crept up. The public peered and pointed like the crowd at St Peter's. Faces turned to him. Was he sick, they questioned? Ill? Dying?

Moving his head was like rolling a giant snowball from side to side. Aching he twisted left and right, searching, and then he saw the ringmaster, back towards him, and he knew with a flood of relief, even before she swung round, that the mannequin was safe and looking after him with that enigmatic smile playing about her lips and that loving look in her eyes that told him not to worry – everything would work out in the end – no despair, always hope.

Jonathan slept through a horrendous thunderstorm. Black clouds obscured the moon and bumped loudly into each other. Vivid white forks of lightning flashed and spat like angry weapons in the celestial battle. Raindrops, each large enough to fill a swimming pool, splattered onto the ground, breaking branches on the trees and creating puddles in the grass. The wind roared and bellowed and smashed windows with pebbles lifted from the driveway. Gloria woke in terror and ran into Henry's room. He, fortunately unoccupied, comforted her with words of wisdom. Electricity was cut off, phone lines torn down. But Jonathan dozed peacefully under the coverlet of goosedown, and the mannequin lay still on the bed in the room next door, her eyes wide open but unseeing and undisturbed.

Andy Pirraner, sent back to his patch in Newcastle, was caught out on his way home from a brothel and ran, drenched and dripping, to the cover of a doorway. It was a newsagent and inside was a pile of last week's *Sunday News*, ready to be collected as pulp. He seethed and boiled with bile as he looked at it. Steam nearly rose from his soaking old coat. Untapped acid can do permanent damage to the nervous system, as the bruises on the skin of the prostitute he had just left sobbing bore witness.

The next day Henry asked to see his employer and sat Jonathan down in the chair opposite his desk.

"I think the time has come for you to review the way I've been managing your affairs, dear. I know financial details bore you, but this is a good moment to occupy your thoughts with mundane matters. So I've organised a meeting with the lawyers and accountants for tomorrow morning. I want you to gather your concentration together and pay attention throughout."

Feeling there was little else for him to do anyway, Jonathan nodded a distracted affirmative. Next day, smartly dressed by Gloria and eased into the car, they swept up to the City.

There is a strange atmosphere in the area behind St Paul's. Utility architecture of glass and steel abounds. Men in three-piece suits with bowler hats and briefcases strut along the street between sensible executive secretaries and crumpled office boys and messengers. Lifts elevate in silence, bereft of the heady strains of muzak. Long-wearing carpets of a discreet tone deaden all but the heaviest footsteps. Doors open soundlessly, conference tables are spotlessly cleaned and gleaming with hard polish. Chairs on wheels glide backwards and forwards. Little tumblers of water remain untouched except by the hands of hired help, pads of legal-lined yellow and sharpened pencils are provided for lethargic doodlers or incomprehensible calculations. Middle-aged women with trim figures like young boys and bifocal spectacles look up cheerily from velvet typewriters. Coffees and teas are fetched in fine porcelain with not quite enough milk and not nearly enough glucose. The blinds on the windows are modern and always half closed. The air conditioning functions perfectly and silently, pumping oxygen-light wind into the air and making the occasional visitor feel as though he's walking on the moon.

This is the world of big business, of tax shelters and corporations, of conglomerates and takeover bids. This is the universe of bankers and brokers, where the numbers are all assumed to be in millions and the newspapers are all pink and rolled for carrying on trains.

"I knew your father well. Started him off, you might say." The elderly gentleman from a very well known firm of investors had been at school with the late Lord Farting. Indeed, he was the very person who had persuaded the merchant bank to assist in those early expansion plans. "Wonderful fellow. Deuced fond of horses. Tragic about him going the way he did. And your mother too. Lovely creature. Great shame. How do you do?"

He extended a shrivelled hand, covered in age spots, to Jonathan, who took it politely and squeezed it harder than strictly necessary. Directors, secretaries, professionals of all kinds graced the table. Jonathan was impressed by the way they all treated Henry with respect. He soon found out why. The annual report, stripped for his benefit of the usual complex jargon and phraseology that so confuses the average intelligent reader in order to convince him that all is well, told a staggering story. Since Henry had grabbed the reins, the assets of the international association had multiplied in value. Stock from nearly every walk of life had been acquired astutely and very few activities had proved unwise. The profits were astronomical. From the initial concentration of interests accidentally achieved by Jonathan's first instructions, Henry had once more expanded and invested brilliantly. The directors delivered a round of applause and rubbed the official figures between their fingers like jewellers with rough diamonds.

During coffee break much cigar breath was puffed up Jonathan's nostrils congratulating him on his choice of chief executive. No reference was made to other activities. Henry took him aside and, looking him straight in the eye, spoke bluntly and specifically.

"My dear, you took me on as a personal assistant but I think you'll agree I've delivered the goods in a spectacular way. Well, now I want to ask you a little favour. One of the more recent acquisitions has been the majority of shares in a certain publication. I'd like you to make me a gift of those shares – yes, me personally – as a reward for my good services so far. It's my birthday next week, so you can think of it as a little present, if you like. I would suggest, if you go along with the scheme, that you announce it in the way of a bonus for my abilities. Even hint that I've turned down some other major offers to stay with you. Now, you know I wouldn't cheat you, dear. These shares are worth several million pounds. But they are a drop in the ocean compared to the increase in value of the corporation since I took over. What do you say?"

Jonathan looked at his friend, so changed from the days in the Selfishes canteen, bright with calm self-confidence, hiding behind no image anymore.

"Will you go on helping me with the other matter?"

Henry's eyes flickered. The world of fantasy seemed distant today.

"I'll do all I can – and anything you want," he said.

So, by a unanimous vote from the board of directors, Henry became the new owner of the *Sunday News*.

The birthday party in Farting Castle. Henry had insisted on a cake with only twenty-one candles and, since the invitation list had, by necessity, to include a great number of old friends, he had partly reverted to his former persona and dressed in a red velvet jacket with a huge blue bow tie. His face, newly creamed with a fresh jar of Bee Pollen Plus, glowed like buttered muffin. They had hired an enormous tent for the evening, which was erected on the lawn against the protests of the gardener who went off and sulked in his potting shed. There were barbecues and Chinese food and roasts turning on spits. Gloria had been put in charge of getting hundreds of glamorous girls to come along and be photographed sitting on Henry's and Jonathan's laps ("Image, dear, must repair the damage"). A fairground had been given the acre at the bottom of the garden and had been paid for a full night of free rides for all guests. "The Affair of the Decade," one national dubbed it. "Top Society Event in Years" blared another. "Aristocracy has Fun" screamed a third. Gossip writers were specifically invited, and a great deal of the hard news section of the international press accepted invitations they didn't get with alacrity when the news about shareholdings in a certain major publishing firm began to leak.

It was a night of much merriment. Gloria and Jonathan had given Henry a private present during the day. On an antique silver platter, worth many thousand pounds, under the solid, carved dome cover, they had placed a single page from a recent issue of the Sunday News with Andy Pirraner's byline attached.

"You see," said Gloria, whose idea it had been, "now you have his headline on a charger!"

Henry moved into Fleet Street very easily. He befriended the unions, raised wages without being asked, mixed with the men on the shop floor and was very popular. Andy Pirraner found his complaint of unfair dismissal rejected extremely swiftly. The change in editor was not difficult to execute, and Tony Schlimer's replacement was well-liked and respected. Clever alterations in paper quality, printing ink and other ancillary costs coupled with the procurement of various distributing units and retail chains enabled Henry to drop the cover price of the *News*. By a cunning swiftness in organising new and advantageous schemes for the union members, he streamlined his work force and became the envy of his rivals, who were still suffering from strikes and overtime bans. He expanded the print order, decreased the size, raised the price of advertising space, spiced up the copy and the layout, stole brilliant writers and photographers from all walks of life and revolutionised the atmosphere. As a result, the *Sunday News*, whose circulation, though large, had been stagnant for years, was wildly successful and enormously profitable.

Andy Pirraner found he could not get another job in journalism due to the union opposition and emigrated.

"Revenge," said Henry one night, "is sweet."

This transformation had taken some weeks and, though he was still living in Farting Castle, Gloria and Jonathan had seen little of him. But he'd not been inactive on Jonathan's behalf and had lined up a series of meetings with intelligent and accomplished men and women who he felt might be able to suggest areas worth investigating. The first of these was a lawyer, specialising in wills, probate, codicils, and the legal definition of life and death. He had prosecuted hospitals for switching off life support units and fought battles for relatives wanting to end suffering loved ones' misery. He had dragged unfortunate abortionists through the courts and had established numerous precedents about the clinical facts of human existence. Henry explained to Jonathan that this man might be able to have the mannequin legally proclaimed alive. If this could be managed, doctors and scientists would have to obey the law of the land and treat her as if she were a human being – which might just, if the right wording was used, force them into providing her with the breath and heartbeat required by the legislature.

Poor Jonathan had not read *Bleak House* or he would never have consented to take steps along that dark corridor leading to the halls of justice. Innocent and naive in the way of judges, juries, solicitors and barristers, he accepted the appointment with alacrity and glee and prepared himself to visit this learned counsel in company with Gloria (Henry being unfortunately too busy to accompany him this time).

It was still summer, but the weather had turned suddenly cold as they set off for Grays Inn. Parking was difficult so they got out some way from their destination and walked. An icy breeze was blowing and they cuddled their clothes around themselves. A churchyard loomed up beside them. Ancient stones, crooked with age, untended graves of unhappy suicides. They turned down a dreary alleyway. Strange men in black flapping gowns and ill-fitting yellowed wigs brushed past carrying enormous leatherbound volumes under their arms. Civilisation seemed to have eluded this pocket of gloom. Soon they found the door, an old wooden barrier studded with metal. They knocked – their bangs echoing on the cold flagstones. Creakily a crabby clerk, well over a hundred years old and stained with ink, opened and beckoned them in. A forbidding waiting chamber like the masters' common room in a very third rate, pre-war public school smelt of crumbling pages and decaying manuscripts. They didn't dare speak to each other, so oppressive was the atmosphere.

"I've got you, now," said the walls, chipped and cracked, stained with tears and sweat and age.

"I've got you, now," said the window, opaque with grime, dust, and dirt.

"I've got you, now," said the floor, chunks of wood uneven and worn by the pleading feet of a million supplicants.

"He'll see you, now," said the clerk, shuffling in and gesturing with his head without looking in their eyes.

They went next door to meet Sir Dimly Vial, QC.

It was a small office for such an important man. Sir Dimly uncoiled himself from behind his desk and offered hands to Jonathan and Gloria. He had very, very long arms and legs and a small body and he never stopped moving his extremities – beckoning, gesticulating, waving, pointing his feet and his fingers, crossing his thighs, bending his knees, exercising his wrists and ankles. He was middle-aged but tidy. His receding blond hair was neatly parted and glued in place with brilliantine. He had very light blue eyes, almost colourless, and a pale, translucent skin. He wore a smart diaphanous suit of a chameleon brown shade. His mouth was large and almost pink and his teeth were creamy and pointed.

"Come into my den," he grinned, and indicated two chairs. "Tell me all, I'm fascinated."

He listened intently as though hoping to hear a fly beat its wings. When Jonathan had finished he picked up a pencil from his desk and Jonathan saw why his teeth were so sharp. A mound of chewed wooden sticks, stripped of paint and splintered down to the lead, lay in the "out" tray.

"This is a strange world, the twilight zone of law," he said, chewing away at the pencil between statements and, sometimes, during them. His voice was high-pitched but monotonous, like a buzz. "We make the mores of society explicit. We write the code that must be obeyed. Many men and women have sat where you are sitting. Murderers, criminals, rapists, thugs. Some I have represented and set free from chains, solely because I believed they were essentially good people. I know the law you see. I am it and I can control it. I know which judge favours which defence. I know who will smile at a prosecution and administer the strictest sentence. You are one of the few exceptions to the rule here. You have chosen to step into our universe of your own free will. Most are forced here by the actions of others."

He leant forwards, touching Jonathan on the knee, waving at Gloria, stabbing the pencil into the gum, smiling and breathing. He scratched a hairless shin.

"I can smell them when they sit there. They are terrified. The sharp odour of fear. And they will never escape. Even if I give them their liberty, they are forever tainted, permanently deformed by the touch of our mitre."

Jonathan cleared his throat nervously. "But do you think you can help me?"

"Oh, perhaps. It's a very interesting case. It will take a long, long time. We shall have to fight it on upwards, appeal after appeal, possibly all the way. But if we win, we shall have broken ground never attempted before. We shall have established a code stronger than any other in existence. Don't worry, it's the sense of history which tempts me to become involved. But the course will not be an easy one, nor a short journey. Prepare yourself to battle for the rest of your life, to challenge the very fabric of society.

"We must analyse the meaning of life. I shall find many celebrated experts who will testify as to what life is – in legal terms. I shall pick the bench, select the magistrates, orchestrate the press coverage and set in motion a public protest in favour of our demands. In itself, that will be evidence. The majority can say something exists, and it does so, in law."

He was becoming excited and had worked through

half a dozen pencils. Stalking about the office, he wound himself around furniture and curled into chairs. He spoke quietly but with emotion. He picked up a sheath of papers from his "in" tray.

"You must sign here. This will contract you to begin the process. It will be frustrating, tiring, aggravating, infuriating. It may go on forever and ever, from musty dock to stale courtroom. One judge will agree, one disagree. But at the end you may have the full power of the law behind you."

He pulled pens from drawers and thrust them at Jonathan, who looked at Gloria. Both of them felt terrified, suffocated, pressurised in this stifling room. Gulping some excuse, he took Gloria by the hand and they ran from the offices out into the courtyard and down the murky passageway into the main street. As they got into the Rolls they were panting and puffing with a combination of physical and mental exhaustion.

"I feel as though we've narrowly missed coming into contact with a fatal infectious disease," said Jonathan. "We could have been talked into wasting all our lives and getting nowhere. Did you see the look in his eyes?"

Gloria was drained. She had seen quite enough of Sir Dimly Vial, QC. Collapsing like an ugly rag doll into the cushions, she burst into tears.

Perhaps all the strain had been too much for her. Gloria took to her room in Farting Castle and refused to come out except at mealtimes. For her role as Greta Garbo she wore black at all times and had bribed the maid to unearth a thick lace veil of the late Lady Farting's which she displayed at dinner and tried to drink soup through. This was messy with consomme and impossible with vegetable. She sighed a lot and placed a hand quite frequently on her ample appendages. Every now and then a tear dribbled down one cheek. At moving moments she would press peoples' arms in a feeling fashion. She knew the woes of the world, the miseries of womanhood. She had been there and come back.

Henry approved of this restrained and gloomy apparition, and introduced her to impressionable business colleagues and future partners. Once he even managed to prise her away from the bedside and guide her around his printing empire. Since virtually nothing could be seen of her apart from a shadowy tangle of material, she created an image of elegance and forebearing which highlit Henry's executive style. Strong men working presses and pumping metal assumed this widow was a beautiful recluse and oozed sympathetic vibrations. Secretaries and hard-nosed journalists sensed tragedy and doom and thought there but for the grace of God went they. A stately ship of sorrow, Gloria found, as many have discovered before her and will do so in the future, that the best remedy for nervous exhaustion is to give in to it completely, wallow in self-pity and weep until the eyeballs are squeezed dry of every drop.

However, Jonathan felt it might be better if she did not accompany him on the next outing arranged by Henry. This was to the cabinet office of one of Her Majesty's ministers. Member of Parliament for a chic north London suburb, Conservative throughout every general election and likely to stay that way.

Henry had apologised about Sir Dimly Vial, QC, but had said he felt his logic was correct, and that the way to push less helpful professions into coinciding with their wishes was to use the weapon of legality. Admittedly, the tangle of red tape and bureaucracy hinted at by Sir Dimly indicated that perhaps the law was not to be utilised so simply, but, even so, if the principle was correct, a clause in a government bill could slip into the rule book in a matter of months. Parliament made the laws; the judiciary merely carried them out; and if the latter body was intent, for its own nefarious purposes, on ensnaring innocent supplicants in a web of complex and expensive niggling, Jonathan would by-pass the instrument and head directly for the manufacturer.

This time Henry agreed to go with him. He'd always wanted to visit the corridors of power, and his contacts had recommended him highly to Veronica Tweed, Home Secretary and a definite candidate for the top job if and when it fell vacant.

Veronica, as she insisted on being called, was honest, straightforward and sincere. She told them that as she was organising cups of tea in Wedgwood china. A handsome woman with long brown hair and smart dress, she was known to have a will of steel concealed behind the attractive façade.

"I've heard the details of your case, obviously, and it strikes me that the easy way out – that of dismissing you immediately – would be unfair and superficial. I don't always believe what I read in the press and I've grown well aware that circumstances are never as black and white as they can be painted. So, please, fill me in with your side of the story and I'll see if I can be of any help."

She sat back and smiled encouragingly. The sun streamed through the bow windows overlooking the Whitehall Gardens. She had done very well for herself. As wife and mother she had proved that being a woman was no handicap. As a career girl, she had climbed the rungs of the political ladder like a well-trained and sensuous monkey. Friendships were abounding, supporters legion. Initially a local organiser for the party, she had literally addressed envelopes and persuaded millions of arthritic but lonely old ladies to do the same. So efficient was she that her promotion had come swiftly and soon she was a fully fledged agent, schooled and taught by the Smith Square experts. All the way along the line she kept notes, names, and numbers in her book, and everyone who helped her was rewarded with a letter or call. When the time came for her to grab a seat for herself, she was given a no-hoper, a certain Labour consitituency where the majority had been in five figures forever. Almost singlehandedly she swept the enormous Welsh borough, learning the language, shaking hands, delivering speeches with a lilting brogue to her voice. The results went completely against the national trend and she came fairly close to achieving the impossible upset. Popular, young and dynamic she had won enough attention to warrant a good, safe seat and she was given it at the earliest opportunity. During elections, she spent her time assisting less guaranteed colleagues in retaining their places in the House of Commons. As many of them said, she was a wonderful woman.

"I can see your point of view," she said, after long, intent listening and contemplation.

"It must be the right of every citizen to choose who to love and to see what he or she wants to see. But the fabric of society is important. By changing a definition in so dramatic a way you could be opening the door to all kinds of social abuses."

"We're only suggesting, Veronica," said Henry, for whom the Minister seemed to have much admiration, "that a phrase or clause could be inserted into a future bill that could be interpreted by experts as – shall we say – commiting scientific assistance to those whose need is valid and who can afford to pay for such services."

"Hm, yes, I see what you mean. So specific as to apply only in extremely limited cases such as your own. . . ."

Jonathan drifted off. The political doubletalk was almost as soporific as Sir Newton Bean's intellectual hypnosis. Henry and Minister Tweed seemed to be embroiling themselves in a froth of words. He stared at them as though through candy floss. A hallucinogenic pink cloud hung over their heads. They seemed to speak with the same voices and move with the same gestures. This was most disturbing. He shook his head to bring back reality but it would not come. The two of them were spinning a huge ball of thread, sticky cotton strands of gossamer emcompassing them both. Then, suddenly, Veronica Tweed snapped out

"Impossible. I would consider that highly immoral. We cannot play with the machinery of government in this way, especially not for concerned interests."

Her voice mellowed again.

"I'm sorry. I didn't mean to bristle. But the fact is that I can't see any way that the majority of motives can be simultaneously satisfied. However, I will put my office onto it. They can examine all the possibilities and there's no reason why some kind of assistance shouldn't be worked out after they report back. Thank you so much for coming to see me."

She proffered a delicate hand and stood up. In the car, Jonathan asked Henry what went wrong.

"I think we were doing all right until I mentioned that the paper would, of course, be supporting the Government at the next election. I should have just let her assume that. Her eyes cleared like wiping film from a diamond and she turned to stone. I suppose she saw the spectre of corruption. Anyway, we weren't really getting anywhere, dear. She was quite prepared to seem sympathetic and intelligent, but she'd never have risked doing anything. Politicians are like that. Good on words, bad on action. You see, the only activities they can promote must appear to be for the benefit of the majority. And, when you analyse the majority, precious little of worth is a common denominator. So you have mere superficialities described as earthshaking developments, and you see civil servants scurrying around like ants building temples out of straw. We are governed by house painters whilst the foundations are rotten with wood worm."

Jonathan had never heard of wooden foundations, but Henry looked so satisfied with his speech that he didn't have the heart to comment. They drove the rest of the way home in silence, Henry smugly delighted with his accurate assessment of civilisation, Jonathan sadly wondering if he would ever see the simple miracle he had spent so much patience waiting for.

In a little bar in Australia Andy Pirraner sipped a beer and thoughtfully waited for the phone to ring. It was freezing in Sydney and he didn't like the place in the least. His job was satisfactory, but his rooms were even more depressing than the ones he'd left behind in Newcastle. Everyone had a silly accent here and used stupid nicknames for each other. Opening hours were strange and short. You had to dodge the customers ricochetting out into the street with an explosion of watery vomit when the pubs closed. And the seasons were the wrong way round. Middle of summer and it was fucking snowing. He'd found ice on his moustache the other day and shaved the whole bloody thing off in irritation. Now he had a clean white line above his upper lip in contrast to the leathery ochre of the rest of his face. His wedge of a nose dripped transparent drops onto it like a leaky pipe onto an old Kleenex. He sniffed, wiped his mouth with a grubby cuff, drank some more of his Fosters and fastened his beady eye on the telephone, bidding it to ring.

They might have been able to drum him out of the business in England, but he still had friends and he had spread some of his ill-gotten gains around useful places. His spy in the *Sunday News* would soon be making a transfer charge call across the world to this number. His rapidly expanding pile of notes on the Farting case would be snapped up soon by an international magazine, when the names got big enough. So far, they ranged from businessmen and working class folk to the Pope and leaders of religious cults. It wouldn't stop there. And Pirraner knew a decent story when he heard one, even if the powers that be had squashed it. Then there was his own personal satisfaction. "Revenge is sweet," he thought to himself, as a sheila with peroxide hair puked over a nearby table, scattering a vast quantity of red prawns in brown ale all over her male companion, who laughed.

That vicious fairy who'd bought the *Sunday News* and turned the very unions against him would be pilloried by his own medium. He, Hatchet Andy, would see to that. If it cost him every penny of the salary he'd earned; if he never worked in newspapers again; if he was dragged into libel cases and bankrupted, he would still have the satisfaction of seeing that pimpled face wiped in the gutter. He picked his nose.

The phone rang and Pirraner leapt to it. His pen was scribbling and very quickly an evil smile lit up his face.

"Nice, very nice," he muttered. "Well, keep your eyes and ears open and call me here tomorrow. I must know everywhere they go. Of course it's in the fucking post," he snapped, and hung up. Veronica Tweed! He'd been longing to get something on her for ages. Now what on earth had happened there in the Home Office? How could he track down some small fragment of truth on which he could erect his monument of fantasy? He buried his nose in his notebook and busied himself on the phone making whispered long distance calls and charging them to his credit card number.

At dinner that night in Farting Castle Gloria had dispensed with the veil and, although still looking severe, she was at least prepared to talk to the others. The long dining table was only ever used at one end, and the vast cavern of a room lay half in darkness. Servants came through swing doors bearing steaming buckets of food. Had they decided to eat at the other extremity of the board, the cuisine would have been cold by the time it arrived. Henry chattered on about plans for a weekly colour magazine giveaway with the subscribers' copies of the paper until Jonathan hushed him and turned to Gloria.

"I think you ought to get out and find yourself something to do. This moping isn't helping at all. You're turning into a zombie. How about visiting your old girlfriends?"

As coincidence would have it, at that very moment the telephone jangled and it was Tracy on the line. Gloria, who had been emerging from her decline and had just begun to find posing as Greta Garbo rather tedious, was happy to assent to Jonathan's advice, with a small show of resistance, and reluctantly agreed to come into Kensington that evening to a party they were going to. Why not bring Henry and Jonathan? Why not, indeed? Henry declined through pressure of work, but Jonathan said he'd escort her and they scampered upstairs to clamber into carnival outfits.

Gloria took some time rearranging her appearance to suit a visit to her old and dear friends. She stripped and plunged into a steaming bath, washing away her agonies in a soapy lather of Camay. The air was humid and hot. She sang a little chirpy number from a Sex Pistols' album. "What the hell. Look to the future, love. Life is ahead of me. I'm still a merry teenager. Now, glamour, glamour, where are you? If you've got it, flaunt it," she mused, polishing her nipples with a face cloth. There was not much she could do about her hair, which, though still short, was irregular and frazzled from misuse over the past weeks. So she washed it, parted it in the middle and sprayed it flat against her head like a lacquer cap. Rifling through Jonathan's late mother's clothes, which she had now claimed for her own, she found a chic, if old-fashioned, grey woolen suit which fitted her perfectly, and a number of simple earrings, brooches, necklaces and bracelets. A touch of rouge on her cheeks and a bright scarlet lipstick splash transformed Gloria the mourning widow via Gloria the sensible wardress to Gloria the fifties vamp.

Jonathan looked much the same as usual.

"Rum and Coke, sport?" Tracy remembered Jonathan well. One of her failures. She eyed him up and down. Not that she'd missed much. About as much sex appeal as a baby kangaroo, blue. The flat was as Gloria had known it, crammed per usual with men of various kinds, bulging at the groin, open at the chest, quick with their hands and slow with their minds.

"How've yer been, Glore?" asked Tracy. Jonathan could see her tongue flapping against her teeth and tried to forget it forcing its way down his throat.

"Depressed, love. It's not been easy, all over the gutter press and home life ruined. But you have to cope, don't you? You do have to cope."

So full was the tiny apartment that Jonathan assumed the party was there. But, no, this was just the girls and their fellas meeting before setting off. And set off they did, mostly jammed into the Rolls but with a fleet of Minis, Volvos, and motor bikes ripping along behind them. The chauffeur, guided by Tracy, who was sitting in front with him, pulled up outside a block of flats in Knightsbridge and everyone spilled onto the pavements, drinks still in hands, shouting and guffawing to each other.

"Ground floor and don't forget the wine," yelled Tracy, and led the way into a maze of rooms packed with merrymakers, noise, music, smoke, and canapés.

Jonathan lost Gloria in the rush and found himself with a glass of dreadful acidic wine in one hand and a stale sausage on a broken toothpick in the other. The overall flavour of the bellowed conversation was Australian but there was an underlying tinge of hippy and some element of Chinese. A couple next to him turned round. The girl was delighted and amazed by life in general, the man had seen it a million times and had always managed to retain his cool.

"Hi, man. Live here?"

"No," said Jonathan, "just visiting with friends."

"Bullshit, man. You're English if ever I saw a pommie in my life, limey bastard."

"Oh, yes, I see what you mean. I am English, yes, but I don't live in London."

The man grunted with bad temper and spilled some wine on Jonathan's shoes. The girl giggled and smiled and looked as though it was all wonderful and wasn't she lucky to be here?

Jonathan elbowed past them with a bland nod of approval and walked straight into a bouncing guitarist. He could tell he was a guitarist because his eyes were closed and his fingers were picking at an imaginary instrument in time to the music on the record player.

"Er . . . sorry . . . er . . . man," said Jonathan, slipping easily into the vernacular.

"Sex and drugs and rock'n'roll," said the guitarist. His eyes conveyed the fact that he had just communicated the formula for life as he knew it. Jonathan looked at him. Perhaps not the finest specimen of humanity, but at least a thriving part thereof, he thought.

"That's where it's at. Dig it! Dig it! Dig it!"

Though limited in knowledge of the current scene Jonathan at least knew that these phrases were some decades out of date. There must be something about Australia, he thought, that causes its natives to develop later than in the rest of the civilised world. As these contemplations were striking him, an enormous crash temporarily silenced the party. The sound was a familiar one. Gloria had inspired another accident.

But no, craning in the direction of the catastrophe

Jonathan saw it was not Gloria at all. An elderly man had leant on the table supporting the bar and record player and managed to tip the entire contents onto the floor. He was flapping about trying to salvage something and the host reconnected the music so the festivities could continue. Jonathan made his way over to the debris.

"Oh, my goodness, I'm so sorry, so dreadfully sorry, I don't know what came over me, I must be mad to sit on so obviously fragile and overladen a surface. Have I ruined everything? No? You have further supplies? Yes, just a shortage of glasses, I fear. No bottles broken. You must allow me to pay for the damage – here, do you think a cheque would be – oh, no, I've left my cheque book at home. How ghastly! What can I do? What can I do?"

The last time Jonathan had heard that voice it was bleating for Mrs Patterson.

"Dr Smooth! How are you?"

"Heavens, a patient. You *are* a patient, aren't you? Or were. Can you help me with this, please? I seem to have snapped – no, it's OK."

He set the table up on its legs and other more competent hands took over. He straightened up and tried to adjust his hair, only succeeding in smearing tomato ketchup on his forehead.

"Now, let me see, don't tell me, you're the man with the fantasy about the nuns – no – I'm wrong – he has a beard. Smith! You're Smith! The underwear sniffer!"

Jonathan felt he should interject rapidly before the entire case histories of all Dr Smooth's patients were made public property.

"No, no Dr Smooth. Jonathan Farting. Remember me?"

"Of course, of course. How nice to see you, my boy. Sorry about all this mess. Your party, is it?"

"No, I'm a guest too. You live just round the corner, here, don't you?"

125

"Indeed. That's why I've come. Always nice at the end of a hard day to relax with old friends and a quiet drink. You seem to be empty. Let me fill you up."

A diligent fellow celebrant performed this duty for the sake of humanity, and gently pushed Dr Peter Smooth into a deserted corner.

"How is your problem?" asked the psychiatrist, who had obviously forgotten what it was.

"Fine," said Jonathan, who felt dishonesty was the best policy under the circumstances. "And you? How are you?"

"Oh, can't complain," said the little analyst. "My brother's been very good to me – recommending patients all the time. You've met him, of course, haven't you?"

"Yes," agreed Jonathan.

"A wonderful man. So talented. So humble. I look up to him, you know."

"Yes," said Jonathan, who knew.

The music was unbearably loud. Something must have gone wrong with the amplifier when it crashed to the ground. As happens on these occasions, the volume of talking rose to match the decibels of music and Jonathan could hardly hear Dr Smooth, who was rambling on, doubtless about his brother's abilities, and wiping his brow on the tail of his shirt which had come adrift during the excitement. All of a sudden the doors burst open and, to the shocked scream of an Australian girl suddenly confronted by visions of official expulsion, a dozen blue uniformed police officers poured into the flat and started arresting people.

Tracy sat next to Jonathan in the Black Maria as they were all driven off to prison.

"Too bad, ain't it, cobber? Just when everyone was beginning to enjoy themselves, too!"

"What happened?"

"Oh, noise complaints, I expect. And then all the drugs and so on. You know what the pigs are like. Can't even have a quiet chunder in London these days."

She was a big girl, well endowed in all the wrong places. Backside like a haunch of venison, forearms like baseball bats, plenty of tusks and a broad flat nose. Everyone said she was the life and soul of the party.

"So, tell me how you've bin gettin' on with that crazy search of yours?"

Jonathan made small talk about Sir Dimly Vial and Veronica Tweed.

"She's Home Secretary, ain't she? Goin' to the top, eh?"

"Yes, but I don't think she'll be any help, unfortunately."

"Really. Why not?"

"Oh, I think she was worried about allegations of corruption and that kind of thing. You know these politicians. All talk."

They were bumping up and down in great discomfort. The windowless van was very stuffy and smelt of sick. Too many people had been thrown into it and arms and legs were poking into the strangest places. Soon they arrived at the police station and were tumbled onto the street and in through the gates. One by one their names were taken and they were herded into communal cells in the basement. Jonathan heard cries of "call my solicitor" and "I'll sue for wrongful arrest" but most went unheeded and he decided he might as well see the adventure through. Dr Peter Smooth was incarcerated with him.

"Oh, dearie me, what shall I do? If this ever gets into the local newspapers, my brother's reputation will be severely damaged."

"I wouldn't worry too much. After all, we weren't doing anything, were we? Just sipping drinks at a rather dreary gathering with a bunch of total strangers."

The unpleasant Australian with the exhilarated girlfriend bumped into him.

"Hey, man. What the fuck is your country doing this for?" he snarled belligerently. Jonathan pretended to look for Gloria.

The guitarist was vomiting in a corner and people were trying not to get too close.

Tracy whispered in his ear. "Drugs, sport. That's 'is trouble. Too much smack."

She didn't *sound* like an Australian, thought Jonathan. More like a cockney with a twang and a slang dictionary.

"Where's Gloria?" he said.

"Dunno, blue. Could be anywhere. Might not 'ave bin picked up at all."

Soon the police started pulling them out one by one. Jonathan's turn came and he was led into a small investigation room and pushed down onto a wooden stool. A man came in wearing a Marks & Spencer suit and a pipe and gestured to a uniformed constable to search him. A very large lump of brown dung came out and was laid on the table. It looked like dried mud from somebody's shoe, and it was followed by a little plastic bag of what Jonathan assumed was icing sugar.

"Not yours?" asked the CID man sarcastically.

"Not mine," said Jonathan, who had guessed by now the route the conversation was taking.

"It's amazing how many people come in here with other people's belongings in their pockets," said the officer. "You'd think Father Christmas had been going around dropping them into empty spaces like presents down the chimney. Oh, well," he sighed, "I suppose we might as well take down your statement, unless you'd like to sign a photcopy of everybody else's."

Jonathan was sweating and dipped into his other

pocket to get a handkerchief. A hypodermic syringe fell out onto the floor.

"Right, sonny boy, we might as well get started."

He was a small man with bright eyes in a cynical podgy face. Putting his mug of coffee down on the table as far away from the cocaine as possible, he slumped into a chair and took out a ballpoint pen which he licked and spread blue ink on his tongue. Shuffled in front of him was an official form in dusty beige with figures and numbers and instructions printed all over it. "Name?" he said.

"May I ask you something?" bleated Jonathan, nervously. He'd never been faced with the full might of society's protectors before and was rightly intimidated. The other policeman looked just like a bobby on the street, safely done up in blue, willing to give the exact time to strangers and to point confused tourists in the direction of Piccadilly Circus. But this man was something else. He seemed so ordinary. He could have been drinking in a pub or sitting next to you in a cinema or cheering on his favourite football team. But an underlying aura of menace crept through his skin as though it was a disguise, a mask. True power gave a metallic ring to his everyday voice. As he lit his pipe with a grimy Swan Vesta match, the gesture revealed a knowledge of supremacy. He was backed by the majority. He was the spokesman for the common factor. It was a different kind of intimidation to that exuded by Sir Dimly Vial, QC. Sir Dimly had created his own power out of the available splinters of civilisation. But the detective was the recipient of total authority. He had, at some stage, decided he wanted to rule other people, and, after a few meagre tests, he had been granted that domination. Overall supremacy in return for asking. Jonathan remembered some of the lesser prefects at the public school who had smelt the same way.

"May I ask you something?" he repeated.

"You'd better make it quick, mate, 'cause I'm about

to charge you officially and, after that, you're on record."

"I was with a girl called Gloria. You don't know if she's here, do you?"

An extraordinary change came over the features of the policeman. The ruthlessness evaporated to be replaced by a combination of understanding, friendliness, furtiveness, and worry. He turned to the constable.

"Go and get me a coffee refill, lad, will you?" He thrust his mug at the young peeler who left the room, closing the door behind him.

"You must be Jonathan, right? I'm Gloria's uncle – her dad's brother John. The boys let her slip away when she mentioned my name at the bust. She said she was there with you and got separated. Well, this is a bit of a problem, isn't it?" He gestured to the pile of evidence on the table. "Not to worry. I'll get one of the lads to lose it somewhere. Well, it's a pleasure to meet you at last. I've heard a lot about you."

He stood up, his bland features creasing into a broad, embarrassed grin. Extending a big slab of a hand, which he first wiped on his trousers, he insisted that Jonathan and Gloria come over to his house for dinner one evening. When the young constable returned he said, "Been a bit of a mistake here, lad," and waved the offending substances into the realm of imagination.

Henry was furious with Gloria. She had returned in the Rolls and removed her makeup and clothes before bothering to wake him up and tell him about the drama. She'd gone to pieces in Italy at the thought of making a splash in the papers, but didn't seem concerned at all by a serious brush with the police. He slapped her a number of times, called her a silly whore and reduced her to tears. Just as he was picking up the phone to summon legal assistance in getting Jonathan bailed, the doors opened and in the

130

prisoner walked with a large bill for a satisfied Pakistani minicab driver.

"Imagine her taking you to that sort of party, stupid bitch," Henry ranted. "If you hadn't been so lucky with a coincidental relationship you'd be all over the papers again, now, and doing a lot of damage to the stocks and shares! Drugs, indeed! Who planted them on you? The fuzz?"

"No, I rather think it was an obnoxious young man who kept swearing at me," said Jonathan. "Anyway, it's all over now – no harm done!"

"There could have been irreparable harm done," said Henry. "I've decided the next place we must go to find a solution to your quest – and that's America. They'd never have let you in with a drugs conviction."

"Why America?"

"Because it's the world capital of the media. You know – films, TV, Disneyland. The structure of U.S. society is built on fantasy. They make Mickey Mouse walk the streets. Imaginary soap opera stars receive more fan mail than the President. That's where we must go – either Hollywood or New York. I'm convinced of it!"

Jonathan was delighted Henry had been spending time thinking about his most important assignment and that fact alone made him clap his hands in glee. He went to bed thrilled by the future and not too concerned about the past. He was awakened by a very early morning phone call.

"Jon, love? It's Tracy. What happened to you? How did you get off?"

His mind was numbed with sleep and confused by her question.

"Off what?"

"The rap, blue. The pigs. We've all just been in court and fined and bound over to keep the bloody peace if we can track the damn thing down. You OK?"

"Oh, Tracy, yes, I'm fine. No problems. Gloria's uncle was in the station."

"Thanks a lot for getting me off too! That's friendship for you!"

"Oh, I'm sorry, but it all got so heavy I only thought about coming home and crashing out."

"Don't worry, Jon, I was only joking. Every man for himself, they always say. Well, at least you got out of the shit without too much crap on you. What you doin' next?"

"Oh, I think we're going to America to chase up the media or something. We'll let you know when we've decided."

"Great. I've always wanted to go to the States. How about taking me with you? Only joking, Jon. Go back to sleep, sport. See you. Bye."

Farting Castle became a tornado of activity over the next few days. Visas were applied for and got, tickets purchased, trunks packed, hotels booked, passports renewed. Feeling bad about deserting Gloria's friend, Jonathan had allowed himself to be inveigled into letting Tracy come along and make it a foursome. She and Henry did not get on at all well, but two boys and two girls looked better for image, so there were no complaints. Henry tried hard to persuade Jonathan not to take the mannequin. He pointed to disadvantageous publicity. He reminded him of their last disastrous overseas travel. He moaned about the difficulty in carrying her. But he'd sown the seeds of his own capitulation. Jonathan was totally convinced that Henry had struck gold this time. The United States of America. Home of opportunity. The land where nothing was impossible, where dreams became reality, fantasy fact. There, if anywhere, lay the answer.

There was a story in the *Standard* that day.

"The brother of Dr Anthony Smooth, the well-known physician, was in court yesterday charged with disturbing the peace, assaulting a police officer, being drunk and disorderly and in possession of dangerous drugs. Dr Peter Smooth, 32, of Walton Street, SW1, was allowed bail at £10,000 on surety of his brother and a Mrs Patterson."

Jonathan felt sorry for the poor man and tried calling him several times. His phone was either off the hook or permanently engaged, but, just as he was giving up, he got a ringing tone and the querulous voice of Mrs Patterson answered.

"Hello? What number are you calling? Who are you, please? What do you want?"

Jonathan explained he was a patient and a friend.

"Oh, it's been a nightmare here, Lord Farting. You don't know what it's like when you get in the papers. They never stop pestering you. Dr Smooth hasn't been taking any calls except from his brother, but I'll ask him if he'll speak to you."

Jonathan heard the phone dropped accidentally on the floor and a table being knocked over before the flustered tones of Dr Smooth started.

"Hello. Oh, my god, isn't it all ghastly? I never thought I'd get out of that dreadful place. How are you? What happened?"

"I'm fine; no problems, I'm glad to say. But how about you?"

"Well, it's been better than it might have been. My brother's been wonderfully understanding and very helpful. He's stood beside me like a tower of strength."

"How about the court situation? The drugs charge sounds rather unfortunate and unfair."

"Yes, grossly so. I'd been filling a prescription for a patient. Should have no trouble proving that. Anyway, I've got an excellent lawyer – another of my patients, as it happens. Referred to me by my brother a little while ago. Went to *him* with lead poisoning. One of the best."

Jonathan began to realise what a narrow escape

133

he'd had. After a few more soothing platitudes he wished the good doctor well and returned to the busy insanity of the castle.

They were due to go that evening for dinner at Gloria's uncle's flat in Chelsea. It proved to be at the end of the Fulham Road in a council estate of highrise towers. The lift wasn't working so they had to climb seventeen floors of stairs and passed some fascinating new obscenities in painted graffiti. Gloria got out of breath at every second landing and crouched wheezing against the concrete bannisters for several minutes, so it took them a long time to arrive at the front door of the flat, and, when they did, they were both drenched in sweat and quite exhausted.

"D'you go through that climb every day?" she asked her uncle after the formal kissing and greeting was over.

"What climb?" he answered.

Gloria's cousins were a sixteen-year-old youth with surly expression, close cropped hair, bright red braces and enormous steel-tipped boots, and a fifteen-year-old girl wearing cheap makeup who kept scratching the inside of her thighs.

"This is Billy," said Uncle John to Jonathan. "Bright lad, though he may not look it. Excellent at sports and all that kind of thing. Backbone of your school, ain't you, son?" He clapped the boy on the shoulder and received a scowl for his trouble.

"And this," he said, "is the pride of the family – little Janice." Janice grinned seductively and scratched a little harder.

"Right – well, kids; now you've met a real Lord, off you go and play. Don't get into any trouble and be back by eleven o'clock."

The two rushed out and down the endless stairs. Jonathan thought he noticed Billy elbowing Janice in the stomach as they went.

A homely looking lady wiping her hands on an

apron emerged from the kitchen with a smile on her face.

"And this is the little woman," said Uncle John. "Supper nearly ready, is it, love?"

The little woman smiled again and nodded and went back to a clatter of pots and pans. They were given a small sweet sherry each and chattered on about America and its potential. Uncle John had his jacket off and there were big, wet sweat stains under the arms of his light blue shirt. His belly bulged over the belt of his trousers, no doubt the product of too many pints of beer shared with informers in pubs.

"He's a sweety, really, love," Gloria had told him in the car. "I've know him for years. Used to bounce up and down on his knees. Could do it without breaking his legs then! I reckon my mum and him had a bit of a fling together once, before she married my dad, of course."

Soon the little woman brought out steaming pots and dishes full of boiled vegetables and roast meats. They sat around a tiny dining table with plastic mats and a neat salt and pepper set made to look like glass flowers.

"The topic" that had brought them into contact with each other was never mentioned, but Uncle John did deliver a sermon on the joys of work, the benefits of the family system and the evils of socialism.

"People don't realise we're all human in the force," he said, "and we're on their side. After all, we're here to protect the majority, aren't we? We may not personally be in favour of things like demonstrations or poofters or women policemen, but the law's the law and it's our duty to uphold it, no matter what."

There was a picture of the Queen on the mantlepiece, and, when Jonathan mentioned Veronica Tweed, Uncle John went off into a paean of praise for her morals, her ethics, her values.

"Marvellous woman. Mind you, I don't generally

approve of them being in men's jobs. But she's the exception that proves the rule, as you might say. Firm and strong. Treats the force in the right way. Fair, that's what she is."

His wife smiled and bobbed in agreement and helped them to some more carrots and cabbage. The phone rang and Uncle John came back into the room with an apologetic look on his face.

"Duty calls, I'm afraid. Worse than being a doctor, isn't it? Massage parlour we've had under surveillance for some time. Must be in on the kill, so it looks like we're going to have to bolt the stuff down a bit sharpish."

Gloria and Jonathan shovelled the food into their mouths like mechanical toys and the little woman ran around hysterically making cups of tea to help swill it into their stomachs.

"Sorry about this," said Uncle John as they stood panting on the pavement. "Anyway, we got to say hello socially, as it were. Perhaps we can get together again when you come back from America! Like your young man," he whispered loudly to Gloria. "Got respect, he has. Not always trying to push his opinions down other people's throats."

He leapt into the police car which was revving its engine impatiently, and shot off into the night. Both Jonathan and Gloria paused for a moment to allow the food to settle like sediment. Jonathan saw half a dozen young thugs beating up a phone booth at the corner of the street. One of them looked rather like Billy.

As they drove home, Gloria started to muse about her life, past, present, and future.

"Funny old world, isn't it, Jon? You think of me, working class girl, brought up by types like uncle John there and mum and dad, ordinary people. And now, all of a sudden, here I am living in a castle with you and Henry and running around the world from

Rome to America. But where's it all going? I mean, I can't keep on sponging off you like this. You've been fantastic, love, letting me enjoy myself without a word of complaint, but it's not right. I know that. Of course, everyone thinks I'm your bird, and that's fine with me, but you and I know it ain't so. Where's that Mr Right, then? I better find him bloody quick or I'll be too old, won't I?"

Jonathan assured her that she wouldn't be, that she was most welcome at Farting Castle and that he regarded her most highly as a friend, confidant, and companion.

"But don't you think of me as anything more, Jon, mate? Don't you ever find yourself stimulated and lonely? Isn't there ever one of those empty moments when you really wish there was a sexy young lady around? Don't I turn you on at all, love?"

She was asking in an enquiring, interested tone of voice, genuinely confused that this seemingly healthy young man should be so untypical of others she had known. Since puberty she had been surrounded by boys whose hands could not avoid trying to run up inside her sweater to grasp the odd mammary and fondle the odd nipple. Jonathan never expressed that healthy desire. Gloria found it very strange. After all, her childhood had been spent reading girlie comics with true love stories in them and gossiping with mates about boyfriends and making herself attractive to the opposite sex and pushing groping fingers away in cinemas.

"You know, I'm not saying if you asked I'd say yes. I think of you as an old friend, almost like a brother. Sex between the two of us would be odd – a bit like incest. But on the other hand, I might be persuaded. You know I've done it, and I have to admit I enjoyed it, even though I'd willingly strangle the little swine now."

She sighed.

"A girl gets lonely, Jon. She likes a bit of male

137

companionship. Most boys your age feel they'd like a bit of female companionship. Physically, at least. Don't you ever get the urge, love? You know, that little twinge?"

"No, Gloria. It's never really bothered me. You have to remember, my heart belongs somewhere else. Now, you might find that a little crazy. I know most other people seem to. But for me it's not. It's important and real and much better than a furtive poke in a car park."

Gloria snuggled into the corner of the back seat with an internal rumble of digesting cabbage.

"Well, never mind, love. We'll always be friends, love, won't we – even if we can't be anything more. And I must say – it has been fun. With the occasional hiccough, of course!"

At that she hiccoughed and they both laughed.

Across the world, Andy Pirraner put the phone on the hook and went back to his dirty table in the Billabong Bar in Sydney. Very interesting. Nearly arrested at a drugs party. Got off because of contacts in high places. Question of corruption in government office at Cabinet level. And still the search went on. His notes were crammed with names, facts, details. Very soon he would be ready to sell an outline of his sensational story to the highest bidder. *Then*, watch out! Andy "Hatchet" Pirraner would be vindicated.

Henry had expanded the *Sunday News* with as much success as he had experienced in the Farting empire. They were launching a national daily as well as taking over an existing London evening paper and his trip to New York was essentially to see if he could acquire the control in one of that city's ailing journals. He rushed around the offices making sure that, in his absence, all would be in capable hands. By now he had trained himself in the ability to delegate, one of the most vital talents of a good chief executive, and he knew that the day-to-day running of creative, financial, and legal areas at the *Sunday News* were well looked after. His complexion, treated during snatched evening sessions with bouts of electrolysis, was almost normal, although it looked rather as if someone had poured porridge in under the skin through tiny micro-surgical slits. He was smart and executive and official. The change during the months had been remarkable. And he had planned expensive nasal reconstruction for his return to England.

Gloria went to London one day and came back as the all-American cheerleader teenage high school girl. Her teeth shone whiter than ever before. Her eyes sparkled with the kind of youthful vitality only ever available from a bottle. Her hair was curled into sexy blonde ringlets and natural waves. Either quick-tan or sessions with a lamp coupled with the natural resources of a fine British summer had given her a healthy, apple red, robust glow and she wore a huge blue sweat shirt with the initial G emblazoned upon it in crimson and the number eighteen embossed on the back. A pleated yellow skirt swung sexily around her thighs just above the knee and she chewed a spearmint flavour bubblegum guaranteed to keep your breath fresh even after eating a clove of raw garlic. Her feet were encased in red, white, and blue tennis boots that came up over her ankles, and her white socks, pulled half way up her calves, were crowned with red and blue stripes.

Henry grumpily commented that he'd preferred her as a widow in black, but smiled when she looked put out, and said, actually, she was rather pretty for a girl, which made her day. Jonathan was amused by the radical alteration and pleased that she seemed back in her old spirits.

The plan was for them to go to New York on Concorde. Henry felt they might as well pay top price and expect top cooperation in return. He'd gone right to the chairman of British Airways and succeeded in getting a command from the top that the mannequin was to be allowed a seat and treated as an invalid lady.

Accordingly, bags were all packed and loaded into the car and the dummy was put in the back with a wheelchair, fully dressed and prepared for her most exciting journey. One of Jonathan's mother's more mature evening gowns draped her slender form, and a hat with a veil obscured the lovely face from inquisitive examination. They set off for London airport, hoping to escape the notice of journalists and photographers when they got there.

THE NEW TESTAMENT

THE NEW
TESTAMENT

No such luck. Leaks always occur, and Heathrow
was a seething nest of photographers and reporters.
Security men cleared a path through the crowds to
the escalator up to the Concorde lounge amidst pop-
ping flashbulbs, glaring TV lights and a howl of questions from indignant commentators. After producing
passports and tickets and accepting blue boarding
cards, they moved into the waiting area, well
shielded, away from the hysteria. Coffee, tea, and a
variety of drinks were available, along with champagne and an assortment of rather wilting sandwiches. The glamour days of supersonic flight were
over, but many an important executive still selected
to fly faster than the speed of sound. It was a mainly
male assortment and approving glances were delivered from three-piece suited businessmen to the
bulging assets of Gloria Miss America. Tracy, bundled up like a large tent, too hot and carrot-coloured
with fluster, was not much regarded. The new ar-
rivals generated a flutter of interest, more amongst
the crew members than passengers, and some whispered comments accompanied the sidelong glances
at Jonathan and his bizarre wheelchair companion.
One smart, middle-aged tycoon put down his *Financial Times* and rushed over to Henry, talking intently about market matters. Henry made a number
of phone calls and looked mildly disturbed.

"I must chat to you about business when we get

to New York," he muttered to Jonathan, before another printing magnate grabbed his elbow and began to congratulate him furiously on his amazing achievements. Jonathan tugged him away and asked him whether he could dampen down the media enthusiasm. Henry thought for a little while and then rushed back to the phone. When he returned he merely said he'd changed his mind and would explain on the plane.

Soon they began loading. Since Concorde is shaped like a cigar tube and is not much bigger than one, regular customers know that unless they sit in the front seats they could take longer disembarking in New York than they took to fly there. Henry, with his contacts, had reserved the first two rows, which gave them more than enough room to stretch and also meant they were the last to get on. One stewardess could not understand why a member of their party so resolutely refused to reply to her polite questions in any way whatsoever, until the chief steward took her aside and explained.

They ate caviar (which Jonathan hated but Gloria wolfed) and drank claret or white burgundy (except for Tracy who was very into rum and Coke followed by a champagne "chaser"). They munched baby quail with grapes and stilton cheese with fragile biscuits which crumbled all over Gloria's outfit. They watched the machmeter reach two to a ripple of polite applause from virgin travellers and then, before they had time to wipe their ice cream flavoured lips with the delicate coffee service, they were on land once more at Kennedy airport where the time was earlier than when they'd set off, the weather hot and humid and the entire news media of the Western world pregnant with anticipation.

The lines had been buzzing from long before take-off. Now, the smutty Pirraner exclusive of several weeks before had grown into a major international story, and the arrival of the innocent boy looking for

144

the secret of life in America, the land of opportunity, had captured the imagination of every suburban housewife and every prole with the ability to fantasise. Henry, aware that the unfortunate angle initially taken by Schlimer and Pirraner had been long forgotten, had decided to be fully geared up to cover the event in his own publications. He'd justified to Jonathan the need for as much publicity as possible by explaining that the media was ruled by the snowball effect, and that the time would come when the item, in order to continue its validity, would have to climax in some kind of drama. That drama, he said, must be the giving of life to the mannequin.

"We've avoided publicity so far, dear, because of the nasty taste of that original piece. But it's swung round now. You're not mocked or derided any more. You've got public sympathy, and the media's going along with that. Let's use it to our advantage."

So the quintet that swept off Concorde into the arms of the picture hungry press was very different to the anonymous group that had slunk on with raised arms and lowered heads. Jonathan smiled and thanked everybody for a wonderful flight, even teased the corner of the veil for the cameras to catch a glimpse of the mannequin's face. Gloria posed and grimaced and bounced at his side. Tracy was happier with the anonymity of Henry's company. Soon they cleared customs and immigration, collected their baggage and gracefully roared out of Kennedy in the waiting six-door Lincoln Continental limousine, towards the multi-storey apartment booked for them in the Waldorf Astoria Towers Hotel.

Andy Pirraner got off his Pan Am standby flight from Australia feeling extremely jetlagged and carrying the odour of babies without house-training. He had been bunched into a terrible seat with broken springs at the very rear of a packed 747, near the toilets, and his stomach churned even more biliously than ever. His room in the downtown YMCA was poky but adequate, and his heart spasmed with pleasure as he swallowed the headlines and saw the full page photo on the front of the *Daily News* and the *New York Post*.

It suited him that they were building up the Farting party as heroes. Further to fall when he released his bombshells. And the bigger they got, the more important they seemed, the greater grew the value of his story.

He chuckled, a dry, raspy hiss of rough air, and picked at a cuticle. Not for long this stuffy cell of a room and this low-level kind of travel. Soon *he* would be the one to fly on first class airlines and wallow in marble baths in luxury suites. But that wasn't ultimately what interested him. It was the satisfaction of ruining the lives of those who had tried to ruin his. He was happy. Happier than he'd been in years. A snarl of pleasure lit up his face.

Joyfully, his finger began to bleed.

The Waldorf Astoria dominates Park Avenue. Restaurants, cabaret rooms, conference halls, and shops spiral off from the tall reception areas; cafés and bars peer into the central meeting places where anxious tourists perch on circular velveteen couches nervously watching their bags. The Towers are the chic rooms and suites, apart from the main body of the hotel, where the rich acquire peace and permanence. Some elderly spinsters and widows actually live in these air-conditioned luxury egg boxes. Other, more transient, occupants can only stand the thin air and reprocessed atmosphere for a limited amount of time. In winter, the heating cracks the paintwork and in summer the icy breezes of air-conditioning widen the splits and peel away the walls, so, as in many New York hotels, the elegance has a dominant tinge of shabbiness.

Newsmen jammed both entrances to the Waldorf as the party arrived. Once more accompanied by dozens of armed security guards, they were rushed in and up to their suite on the thirty-fifth and thirty-sixth floors. Jonathan felt quite dizzy in the elevator and Gloria began to have palpitations. Henry turned on one of the colour TV sets and caught some of the coverage. They were definitely regarded as celebrities. A fat-faced coloured lady with a permanent grin was reading details about their arrival from an autocue with a patronising twinkle in her eye. He switched channels. An elegant newscaster was joking about them to a giggling weatherman. He twisted the knob once more. A jolly sports commentator had managed to include a mention for them in his coverage of a Mets game.

"We must be sure to ration our appearances," he said. "Too much too soon could be as disastrous as none at all."

The mannequin was installed in a large bedroom overlooking Lexington Avenue. She lay on the green and white embroidered coverlet, fully dressed for her next outing. Gloria and Tracy were sharing another room and unpacked with great excitement. They made full use of room service and had trays bearing alcohol and snacks delivered every few minutes so they could assess the assets of the waiters. The two of them were like schoolgirls, chattering and prattling with merriment.

Henry had already planned a full diary of meetings and conferences for himself and a few useful contacts for Jonathan. One of these was the top New York publicist. He was a sleek, amusing young man whose reputation preceded him. Responsible for the election to office of numerous state and city officials, he had recently represented a presidential candidate in his quest for the ultimate post, and though not successful in the final result, had correctly assumed great credit for acres of coverage and miles of press cuttings. Originally, in the world of popular music, he had masterminded trends and established fashions which still influenced the market place.

"This is a most exacting mission," he said. "If you decide I'm the right man for the job, I shall give up my other campaigns and devote my skills entirely to your service."

He smiled superficially and sipped his black coffee.

"You've read about me, I'm sure. You know my track record. I don't think I have to sell you on my abilities. It will be a question of chemistry. If you and I, Lord Farting, gell together; if we spark off each other; if I can understand your motivation and you can believe in my comprehension, we will make a formidable team."

David Kraft was handsome and sharp. He had tight black curly pubic hair covering his body except for his head, which was polished brown mahogany. He shaved at least five times a day but his skin had the rough darkness of somebody who had lost the battle against pellicules. His eyes were like a squirrel's, bright and brown, darting from place to place with instant observation. Charm and sincerity were weapons in his arsenal. The ultimate salesman, hard to spot as anything other than a genuine and talented public relations man, he was fascinated by the media and manipulated it as much as he could.

"You are right," he said to Henry, "the secret is rationing. We can get massive coverage by leaking pieces of information bit by bit. My organisation can control the areas of disclosure and the direction of exposure. We must aim to get the public so well informed about the campaign that the television networks will beg us for an exclusive special about you. Then we dictate our own terms."

"Is it possible?" asked Jonathan. He knew he was dealing with a professional here, and felt relieved to have one on his side at last.

"Everything is possible where the media is concerned," answered David Kraft. "I have manufactured

148

groups of pimpled, talentless homosexual teenagers and turned them into the idols of every young girl in America – even the world. I have taken corrupt and insane local politicians and whitewashed them into congressmen. I have formed and shaped unknown senators into governors and, very nearly, presidents. But your account will bring me the most satisfaction. To introduce a lifeless mannequin to the world of television and force the barons of the media to spirit her into a living, breathing human being – yes, that is a challenge I shall relish."

Jonathan grew more and more excited as Kraft spoke. Henry, too, was feeling the infection of enthusiasm.

Financial details completed, David Kraft left the suite promising to return the next morning with a specific game-plan and blueprint for his forces to follow.

"This is it, Henry. I can sense it," said Jonathan, flushed with pleasure. "The end of an impossible dream."

"Well, I hope so, for your sake, dear," said Henry, with less scepticism than usual. "Now – we must discuss some minor details about your empire . . ."

"Not at the moment, Henry. I want everyone to concentrate on this one goal. Too many topics will disseminate the vibrations. Just let me give my entire attention to this."

Jonathan left the room and went to sit with his beloved. Henry sighed and returned to his delicate negotiations with attorneys for the New York publication. Gloria and Tracy were already out seeing the sights, going up the Empire State Building, sipping cocktails in the Windows on the World restaurant atop the Trade Centre, spinning in and out of potholes in a legion of yellow cabs.

Andy Pirraner had found an all-day singles bar and was drinking Scotch and ogling the lovely female patrons, wondering which, if any, would be turned on by a session of masochism.

"Hi, Jon, this is Alexis. We met him in Washington Square."

Alexis was a smooth man in a fashionable check suit with a gold snake curled around his neck. Gloria hung on his arm.

"Alexis owns a chain of sex shops here in Manhattan. Makes a fortune out of them. But we mustn't talk about them too much. Something to do with the IRF or IRX, isn't it, Alex?"

"Yes," said Alex.

Alex bulged in unfortunate places with shapes and contours of a lethal nature. Alex would not take off his jacket and seemed the strong, silent type. Alex could have failed a metal detector test.

"Alex said you're to come with him for a tour of his establishments. I said I wouldn't go unless my fella could come too." She winked at Jonathan with a very unsubtle gesture.

"You will enjoy," said Alex, more as a command than a statement.

"Tracy's already gone off with Alexis' friend Gino. We're meeting her there. Come on, Jon."

Jonathan felt this was altogether an unwise expedition, but, since Tracy had obviously succumbed to the other man's blandishments, he thought it would be unchivalrous to desert her. He tried to get in to Henry to tell him where they were going, but a top level meeting was in heavy progress and all interruption barred by the efficient hired secretary, so he left a note and went downstairs with Gloria and Alexis. There was no chance of a quick word with her on the way since she seemed glued to her new boyfriend's arm, but she didn't appear unduly disturbed by the circumstances, only extremely tipsy, so he kept his fingers crossed that they weren't walking into trouble.

Alexis was driven by a person with a harelip in an old Cadillac with artificial fur seats, black windows and gilt accessories. They turned down 42nd Street and coasted up to a garish red and yellow shop called Playdate with flashing neon signs proclaiming "Live sex acts for 25c".

"Are you sure Tracy's come here?" asked Jonathan.

"She with Gino. Private flat at back. Very nice. You see."

They walked through the shop past numerous men of varying ages looking anonymous and stimulated who were fingering glossy books and plastic sex aids with medical expressions on their faces. A series of little doors with red lights above them indicated the booths were collecting the 25c for a minute or two of prurient observation as a couple copulated mechanically on a revolving circular bed. Alexis slipped a key into a lock and they were out of the shop onto a darkened stairwell, through another door, and sure enough, an entire apartment lay concealed in front of them, furnished in tasteful Carmen Miranda style with plenty of plastic fruit, convertible sofas, and inflammable flowered curtains made of cheap polyester. Tracy was occupied by a young Puerto Rican in a session of mutual oral stimulation. She was obviously extremely drunk.

"Hello, Gino," said Jonathan.

"Not Gino, Pedro," said the offending youth, returning to his animated liplicking.

"Gino," said Alexis, gesturing towards a large Italian in tight slacks combing his hair in an ornamental mirror.

"Hi, Jon, sport!" cried Tracy. "Fantastic party, blue."

Jonathan couldn't see the party, but assumed Tracy adhered to the belief that any gathering over two conformed to that description.

Alexis began to cuddle Gloria and Jonathan was

feeling rather left out when a door opened and a middle-aged entrepreneur walked in, flanked by two menacing hoods. A conversation in a foreign language between him and Alexis took place in heated tones, then he sat down and motioned to Jonathan to sit next to him whilst the disturbed affection continued.

"They are really not allowed to pick up young tourist ladies," he said, in perfect English, although he looked Arabic. "But the girls seem happy, so who am I to curb their pleasures? They are only children, these boys. As long as they do their jobs, they can relax for a few moments. The situation is all right with you, I hope? We're not walking on forbidden ground?"

"No, no, not at all."

"I wouldn't want visitors to consider us gangsters. People like myself who run legitimate businesses have a dreadful image with the average man on the street. They believe that we're all Mafia run or connected with some international crime syndicate or other. Not true at all."

He pulled out a gold toothpick and casually removed a seed from between his teeth. Around them, Gloria and Tracy were giggling and frolicking with much merry laughter and friendly hand-slapping.

"There is a need for us, and we try to provide release in as clean and healthy a way as possible. Nice, attractive pictures. Inflatable dolls, electric organs, stimulating films. Nothing unpleasant. No real violence – except acted, of course. Photos of animals and children and so on, we provide only for the specialist. We are very moral people."

One of his bodyguards shifted on his feet with a low, soft grunt of muscle movement. Tracy squealed a phony protest as Pedro tweaked a nipple.

"Think of all the rape and molesting that would go on if we didn't allow frustrations to spurt out in harmless activity. All that pressure mounting up in testicles. All those fantasies unfulfilled. We are an outlet, my friend."

He patted Jonathan's leg and breathed a blast of stale warm wind into his face. He had crinkly grey hair and skin like pumice stone. His eyelids were very heavy, his nostrils very round.

"So, when you go back to England, pass on the word that we're not as bad as we look. I have businesses in London, too, you know. Very profitable, very socially beneficial. You will find a Playdate shop in most of the world's capitals."

A telephone rang and one of the shadows answered it and nodded to his chief, who took the call, listened quietly, came back and sat down once more.

"It has been a pleasure talking with you. I hope you enjoy your visit to our beautiful city."

He looked at his Cartier watch, stood up and barked an order to his employees, who shot to attention, buttoning up clothing. Tracy and Gloria, muddled with drink, were bundled back down the stairs and into the Cadillac. At the Waldorf they were pushed out onto the pavement without a word (Alexis, Pedro, and Gino had not spoken since their boss had snapped out his instructions) and staggered ruefully up to the suite.

"Well, blue, what a drag. It was just beginning to be fun," complained Tracy.

Henry was waiting for them with a burly, official man who looked like an American version of Gloria's Uncle John.

"You stupid girls! What do you think you were doing? This is Lieutenant Parker of the NYPD."

Parker told them that the Playdate club had been under observation for months. The pleasant dealer Jonathan had spoken with at length was a well-known gangster with a number of suspected murders under his belt. Alexis, Gino, and Pedro were hit men, hired killers, assassins and villains. Sometimes they

153

bought and sold drugs. They were thought to run several teams of prostitutes in the area.

Gloria sat down.

"Your friend here was worried by the address you left for him and phoned us at the precinct. You're quite lucky to be here. One of the boss's contacts at the station must have called and warned him we were coming over. Otherwise, two of you would be working the streets of Rio and you, Lord Farting, would probably be wearing concrete boots. It happens all the time."

Tracy sat down too.

When Lieutenant Parker left, Henry was obviously about to deliver one of his moral lectures and Jonathan felt he had to remind him that his own past exploits had been dubious, to say the least. Henry was outraged at being reprimanded and commented that it was Jonathan who had refused to discuss serious business matters because of wishing to think about one specific subject only.

"I can't see how rushing off to visit the sewers of New York will contribute in any way, darling," he bitched, retreating to his roots as the atmosphere tensed. "You might have been killed, or, at best, busted again in a den of iniquity and that would have done the cause no good at all! How do you think I felt when I got a note saying you'd gone to meet some men at Playdate Sex Shop?"

Gloria was in tears by now and Tracy had slumped into a comatose bundle on the fake antique loveseat. She looked like a depressed water buffalo paralysed by a dart. Gloria managed to break a vase, two lamps and a writing desk on her erratic way to a hot bath and bed, but she recovered her good spirits soon enough whereas Tracy seemed to have suffered a mortal blow and remained silent and morose, all the stuffing gone out of her like a toy wallaby at a jumble sale in the outback.

The blitz on the media had started. David Kraft had briefed Jonathan in absolute detail about the way to look, behave, speak and be interviewed. He had insisted on Jonathan having a total facial treatment at a well-known British beauty parlour and had personally overseen his haircut and choice of wardrobe at Barney's English department. Jonathan did several tightly scripted TV chat shows where Kraft insisted on controlling lights and camera angles, having a look at all questions in advance and refusing to allow other guests into his segment. He succeeded in building up an aura of tragic mystique that titillated Americans to near orgasm and brought network executives to his phone in droves. No, he would not allow Lord Farting to show the mannequin to anyone, just yet. No, he would not allow Lord Farting to guest spot on various assorted TV cop shows. Yes, he was prepared to discuss the proposal of a special built around Lord Farting, but only on his own terms, and you couldn't afford them, I'm afraid.

Housewives fell deeply in love with this tragic British Lord, so alone and so sad. He was named in divorce suits. Bars were emptied when he was on television. Radio programmes begged for his encapsulated thoughts and ran them relentlessly during all shows. Badges proclaimed "Jonathan for President" and T-shirts shouted "Love is a mannequin".

Kraft would not let success and hero worship deflect him from his goal. He had many a meeting with Henry and Jonathan (twice, incidentally, turning down offers of jobs in the fast-growing *Sunday News* conglomerate). Again and again he repeated the formula.

"Do not let the mania go to your head," he said. "If you want the results we agreed, you must weather this hurricane of popularity."

His scheme involved Jonathan criss-crossing the country on a tour of local news shows before finally demanding the network special.

"And I think I know who we'll go with," he said. "The most trusted living American – not only is he the front man for a magnificent nightly talk show, but he is the founder and president of the number one network in the country. His name is Abe Pursen, and if anyone can work a miracle, he can."

Kraft was watching the timing factor. The story he had nurtured so well must not be allowed to bore the public. He had hired a number of well-regarded pollsters to measure the national reaction to Jonathan's quest in terms of awareness, sympathy and so on. These hard-working ferrets had teams of volunteers phoning random numbers, used controlled mail shots in bulk and every other trick to discover Mr and Mrs Average's attitudes. So Jonathan was shunted from city to city, hotel to hotel, dramatically conveying the same misty-eyed message of love and sadness; justifying his reason; pleading, with dignity, for support and understanding.

Andy Pirraner had written the greatest story ever told. A number of national weekly scandal rags expressed hungry interest and offered large sums of money. The negotiations were conducted in gravest secrecy and eventually finalised between Hatchet and the editor-in-chief of the *National Star*, a colour tabloid specialising in stories about fatal illnesses in glamorous celebrities, sexual exploits of pop stars and actresses, photos of freaks, and predictions by vain and incompetent astrologers. Rightly, therefore, they had a large circulation.

Simultaneously, David Kraft had clinched the deal with Abe Pursen at ABS Television. Jonathan was to have a two-hour special at prime time on a Saturday evening, pre-empting one of the network's most popular soap operas.

Abe was a wise, generous, sincere man in his middle fifties or early seventies with a wave of fine white hair and a permanent suntan. His blue eyes could blaze with righteous indignation or soften in love and pity. His voice could trumpet like an evangelist or rumble with deep power like the word of the Lord. His handshake was firm and strong yet gentle and soothing. Jonathan loved him immediately. Millions of Americans did too.

"That's the way it is, young man. I can't promise a miracle, but I can and will try. We shall invite the most powerful men and women in the nation to come to the studio. We shall urge Americans everywhere to pray for you. We shall stage a show around you so wondrous that people will talk about it for decades. We shall rerun flashbacks of nostalgia to illustrate how much the media has accomplished. We shall remind the viewers of the mightiest feats of man – electricity, the airplane, penicillin, the telephone. If anything can triumph over logic – we can."

His office was vast and panelled in elm wood. His desk was immense. His personality impressive and gigantic. Jonathan was imbued by a feeling of elation. The summit of his tribulations, the climax of his life, the apex of his desires! The date for the special was set for three Saturdays hence, and the advertising campaign was set to roll. David Kraft was satisfied. Jonathan was delighted.

Abe Pursen was not his real name. His parents were a Jewish-Ukrainian couple who had emigrated to America and started a bakery. Swiftly, in the lower East Side neighbourhood of New York, the delicious cakes, breads, and ethnic confections became staple diet for those who could afford them. His father opened other stores. Soon a chain existed. One day, whilst his parents were on holiday in Coney Island, and Abe, then Abraham, was in charge, he made a decision to advertise on the sickly new medium – radio.

His father, finding, on returning, that his teenage son had spent several hard-earned dollars on such an absurd venture, beat him to within an inch of his life (the family was very strict). His mother, tears in her eyes, intervened and pointed out that sales had increased by six hundred per cent over the fortnight. Father sternly admonished her, reciting Biblical passages and illustrating that it was the principle which mattered. He then beat his wife to within an inch of her life (it was, indeed, a very strict family).

However, he continued to advertise on the radio and for Christmas gave little Abraham his own bagel stand.

Abe felt, however, that his future did not lie in dough and sesame seeds. He sold the bagel stand and banked the profits. He took on a series of menial, well-paid jobs, including sewage cleaning and packing contraceptives in an international firm's factory where he was paid for quantity achieved rather than quality of work. His savings grew rapidly. Soon he had enough to buy a radio station. It was a small, ramshackle place, but it was a start.

The rest is history. Radio became television and the good-looking leader of the rapidly-expanding Abraham Broadcasting Services network, or ABS for short, became the hero of the media. Throughout all this, fascination with the power of his acquisitions forced him to continue in a front man position throughout the years. And, unlike other hosts who fall into disfavour and retire to hotels in Miami, he retained and even increased his hold on the audience.

"He is highly regarded as the most powerful man in the world," said David Kraft. They had returned to Jonathan's suite and were quietly sipping Earl Grey tea and nibbling chocolate chip cookies, possibly manufactured by a distant relative of the deity they were discussing.

"I feel so stupid. I've wasted so long going from clown to clown, expert to expert, and I should have just come straight here. I'm very grateful to you," said Jonathan.

Kraft smiled and crossed a neatly-creased trouser leg revealing a jungle of curly hair at his ankles.

"I don't think you're stupid at all. I think you've been very brave. It's not often someone is prepared to have the courage of his convictions. I studied law at Harvard and mastered the art of accountancy, but I, too, knew that the true direction for my life led elsewhere. So I threw it all up and went into the music industry. Even there, when I was begged to become president of a major record company, I realised that what I most deeply enjoyed was the actual achievement of taking on challenges and beating the odds. So I went out on my own and here I am. You, for instance, could have settled for being a country squire on your estate in England, or an industrial tycoon at the head of vast conglomerates. But, no, you have devoted your life to searching for a Holy Grail. And now it may be within your grasp."

Henry walked in with folders under his arms and a pen behind his ear. He greeted Kraft with a nod and turned to Jonathan.

"Jonathan, I really must insist we spend some time going over your business affairs. There are areas of decision which I *must* have your opinion on. For instance . . ."

"No, no, Henry. Not now. We have fabulous news. The TV show is all lined up. It's going to go on air in three Saturdays' time."

"Fantastic. Congratulations," he said to David Kraft, shaking his hand. "Even so . . ."

A secretary rushed in and bleated platitudes about American Print Unions and the mayor's office being on the phone. Henry apologised and went out.

"He's a very able man," said David. "Where did you find him?"

"The same place I found the mannequin," said Jonathan. "Would you like to see her? I think you've earned it."

"No, I feel it would be better for me to remain

159

objective. Involvement might lead to cynicism. I will see her when everyone else does."

Kraft was delighted the way things were going and did not fancy ruining his enthusiasm with a blast of reality. His reputation was more enhanced than ever. Whilst the public was begging for Jonathan, industrial leaders could spot the power behind the scenes and David Kraft had acquired a number of major new accounts. Soon he would be a millionaire. He smiled graciously.

Preparations for the show unwound steadily. Jonathan was surrounded by researchers, directors, designers, floor managers and all the paraphernalia of modern creation. When he could, he went out with Gloria and examined the city. They craned their necks to see the chunk of blue sky sandwiched between the skyscraper crowns. They avoided the drunks and crazy bag people with matted hair and filthy rags who seemed to populate the streets. They travelled on the multicoloured subway trains, beneficiaries of millions of dollars of spray paint, and drove out to New Jersey and Long Island. They examined the Brooklyn Bridge and Chinatown and Little Italy. Quite often they walked to the large ABS studios, situated on 57th Street in a disused theatre, and gazed in awe at the mammoth set of steel girders and fantastic backdrops. This would surely be the biggest and best ever.

Andy Pirraner was at the final stage of his exclusive revelations. The *National Star* had decided to run his piece in their issue released the day after the TV show aired. Massive protective precautions were taken. The cover art would be delivered personally to the printers by the editor. Advertising departments were kept away from sheets of blank pages allocated to the confidential report. To celebrate his coup, the Hatchet went to the most expensive and elaborate East Side brothel, a plush brownstone house on 75th Street, selected the most beautiful and well-endowed young lady in the establishment, took her to the top private suite there and, over a mouth-watering repast of haute cuisine, beat her to pulp and gave her wounds and scars that increased his bill by several thousand dollars for radical plastic surgery expenses.

The big day crept closer. Billboards in Times Square announced the show; brilliant commercials interrupted network news. The rival TV channels gave up the battle and scheduled re-runs of the *Mary Tyler Moore Show*.

It was Friday and the suite was a proverbial hive of activity. Makeup artistes and dressers measured and shaded and squinted and squealed. Gloria had decided that a change of image was needed for the main event and had deserted the cheerleader style for the modern model girl look. Her body was strapped into slim-fitting casual wear, her hair tortured into a giant black Afro cut which frizzed and sizzled like the mane of an electrified lion. Possibly the strands were complaining about this constant dying and bleaching they were suffering. With the new coiffure she was several inches taller and towered above Jonathan like an elegant, if wobbly, stilt walker.

"How d'you like it, Jon, love?" she asked.

"Fine," he answered.

Tracy was, if possible, even more maudlin and depressed than before. Her eyes were red and swollen with crying and her inattention to her physical appearance meant she looked like a moose preparing to become extinct at any moment. As the day turned to evening, she begged Jonathan and Gloria to attend her alone in her room and, when they arrived, burst into choking sobs.

When she'd been comforted and soothed into a cogent state, she stammered out her dreadful confession. She'd received a call from Australia some weeks ago. It had been Andy Pirraner. She'd almost hung up on him, but he'd offered her a large sum of money to track down some information. She'd given him her bank account number and been amazed to find three zeros at the end of her balance the next day. Since she'd resented Gloria deserting her old friends, she managed to convince herself that she would be paying her back for her thoughtless behaviour. But she knew it was really for the money.

She collapsed in misery again and took some time out to chastise herself with every known swear word before the others had a chance to do so.

So she'd phoned Gloria up and taken it from there, filling Pirraner in with every development once a week. Gradually, as they were all so good to her, she'd felt worse and worse about her behaviour. Then came the sex shop fiasco, when they'd rescued her from the jaws of wolves. That had really done her in. Crushed by the knowledge that she was a Judas in their midst, she had made only one more phone call, and it had revealed that they were all to be exposed in that week's *National Star*.

This was terrible news. Jonathan rushed into Henry's room but he was out at a meeting in some secret restaurant, no one knew where, conducting the final stages of his takeover bid.

Jonathan and Gloria talked about it. There was no point in crying over spilt milk, they decided, and, anyway, the paper would not be out until after the TV show. By then, all would have been lost or won and vicious allegations could do no harm. Better to keep it all quiet and continue as planned. Gloria was nervous about personal repercussions but racked her brain and could find no further blemishes in her conduct that Pirraner could possibly expose. So they consoled Tracy with sweet words and determined to shrug their shoulders and let the show go on.

Saturday dawned with the drama forgotten. Jonathan almost mentioned it to Henry but didn't, as he was so triumphant at having signed the deal solidifying his ownership of the prestigious, if impoverished *Wall of Commerce Journal*; an ancient, highly respected New York publication read by intellectual stockbrokers but rather behind the times in layout, format, and attitude.

"It will give me a whole new marketplace," he said, "and, if I'm clever, we can multiply circulation as well as retaining the quality subscriptions we have."

"Wonderful!" said Jonathan, excited by more pressing matters, but pleased for his friend.

"We must have that business talk, dear; it really is getting very important."

"Tomorrow, Henry. When we're there."

No doubt existed in Jonathan's mind that the TV show would be a success. Not only as a programme, but as the element needed to achieve his goal. In truth, nobody else went along with this positive certainty although many optimistic nods and affirmative grins persuaded him they did. The general opinion was that it would be a spectacular and rewarding two hours of television created on a premise of lunacy.

Only Abe Pursen had the honesty to tell Jonathan that he was hoping for a one-in-million chance.

"I would never be so foolish as to say miracles cannot happen. With all my heart I wish that this one can. But you must prepare yourself for disappointment just in case."

Euphoria ruled, however, and Jonathan had been instilled with belief, a dangerous drug at the best of times. So they arrived in their limousines at the theatre. Thousands packed the streets outside. Police had closed off the entire area – several blocks wide – and diverted traffic to the most obscure routes. As Jonathan walked towards the doors, shouts of support and solidarity rang out in a hundred voices. The young man pushing the wheelchair was almost blinded by flashing lights and glaring beams. Microphones sprouted for actuality like triffids. Householders leant from windows and hurled confetti. Streamers and balloons and banners flew over their heads. It made Academy Awards' night look like a funeral for an unknown drunk.

They were inside and guided to their seats on the stage. The mannequin, simply but beautifully gowned in exquisite taste, was veiled for the moment. She sat on Jonathan's right in a golden throne created exclusively at great expense to the ABS shareholders. Abe Pursen, dignified and proud, relaxed on a swivel chair in the centre of the set. The audience filed in, quiet and respectful as though they were in church. Doctors, politicians, scientists, executives, intellectuals, psychics, priests, and lawyers ranged around, culled at enormous cost from the finest universities and colleges in the land. The minute hand hit twelve and the show began.

The orchestra struck up a grand concerto of brass, strings, keyboards, drums, and guitars. Then a lone piano played a simple, moving melody in a minor key. The contrasts in power and grace overwhelmed the audience, some of whom openly wept. Then Abe Pursen, camera zooming in, stood up and delivered his speech. It was regal, moving, magnificent. He was tall, dignified and commanding. His resonant voice recalled greatness past, and painted promise of the future. A striking lady in a sweeping sequinned dress sang the national anthem, and a brilliant montage of old film clips, newsreel moments, and international crises swept across the huge screen behind the stage. Lights lasered in and out of the crowd; scents and odours were sprayed amongst them, flavouring their senses subconsciously with their subtle smoke. Experts moved one by one to the giant carved pulpit and delivered passionate exhortations. Top performers combined their greatest hits with new words praising the event and surpassed each other in superb exhibitions of heart-string tugging.

The two hours were commercial free – unheard of in American television. Special dispensation had been granted by the FCC to increase the size of spots either side of the special, so the atmosphere would not be disturbed and the vibrations could concentrate on the nativity. Eventually, after a feast of great paintings, wonderful music, fine homilies and natural, ad-libbed, well-rehearsed moments, Jonathan's turn came.

To a hush from the audience he walked to the lectern and raised his eyes to the camera. His words were sweet, sad, desperate, noble, humble, and proud. Written by David Kraft, they represented one of his finer releases. Jonathan spoke them in a near whisper, his voice throbbing with emotion. Then Abe Pursen stood up again. To Jonathan he appeared taller, mightier than ever. Somehow he had changed into a radiant, white flowing robe. He raised his arms, calling the universe, challenging the planets, commanding the forces of the galaxy. Fireworks exploded, special effects transformed the theatre into a moving rocket. The musicians hammered their instruments in a frenzy of excitement. Two aides stepped forward and approached the dummy. Jonathan moved nervously. Should he let them touch her? A fear took control of his heart, freezing him to ice. The aides grasped a corner each of the veil and raised it over her head.

She was quite rigid, motionless, exactly as he had last seen her. Still as beautiful, still looking at him, giving him the message with her soft eyes. "Believe."

His heart surged. He would not allow himself to betray her. She *would* live – he willed it!

The disappointed sigh from the audience turned into a gasp of disbelief. Slowly the mannequin moved. She lifted her head and smiled – a sweet, enigmatic, glowing expression. She took her hands from her lap and stood up, tall and distinguished, imperial and radiant. Jonathan rushed forwards. He couldn't accept it. Now it had happened, he couldn't believe it. Voices shouted, the atmosphere was electric. Only Abe Pursen remained calm and unmoved. Jonathan grabbed the mannequin's arm and looked for the little nick which had been chipped from her body all those months ago. Nobody else knew about that. It was his safeguard against trickery, substitution, deceit.

It was there. Exactly as it had been, impossible to duplicate, the tiny triangular dent.

"It's her! It's really her! She lives!" he cried, and fell to the floor in front of her, unconscious in his happiness.

So ended the most spectacularly successful television show in the history of the glowing tube.

THE BOOK
OF REVELATIONS

THE BOOK
OF REVELATIONS

Jonathan woke up in a dark dressing room.

"Hello," said the mannequin.

"You're really here. Is it you? Tell me the truth, you aren't a phony, are you?"

"Didn't I always tell you to believe? Of course it's me. I knew you'd get me here if you persevered. I really have to thank you. And Mr Pursen, of course, without him it wouldn't have been possible. But you were the one with the faith. You kept going when everyone pressurised you to give up. I'm extremely grateful. Life as a mannequin would have been very boring."

"This is wonderful," said Jonathan. "It's a miracle."

"Yes, indeed. The first time, though certainly not the last. Now they've done it for me, everyone will be wanting it. I don't suppose you know what you've started. That's the problem with naivety. Never looking ahead. Just accepting the present and blundering on. Still, I can't complain. You've done well by me, Jonathan. I shall be permanently indebted to you."

Jonathan was beginning to feel a trifle uneasy. He put it down to the bump on his head when he fell.

"You've learnt to speak very well, considering."

"Considering what, may I ask? I might have been a dummy all my life but that doesn't mean to say I can't observe and listen and absorb, you know. A great deal of information is residing in this little head, honey, believe me."

She stood up and began pacing around. "Got a cigarette?"

"Sorry, I don't smoke."

"Oh, I forgot, of course you don't. Never mind."

She opened the dressing room door. "Tracy! Get me some fags, will you, love. And tell the others his Lordship's conscious again."

"How did it happen?" asked Jonathan, by now extremely disturbed.

"Oh, vibrations basically. Just a question of getting enough people thinking and feeling the same thing at the same time. A man can move a mountain, I believe someone once said. Well, now I've passed on my thanks I'd better be going. I've got clothes to buy and roots to put down. I'll see you back at the Waldorf in a few hours. Don't happen to have any dollars on you, by any chance? Oh, no, of course – you only carry credit cards. Never mind, I'll scrounge it off Henry. See you later, love. And thanks again."

She leant over and plastered a sticky wet kiss on his cheek. Grabbing the packet of Marlboro from Tracy with a grin as she left, she swept down the corridor acknowledging the respects of awestruck mortals on her way.

"She certainly is beautiful, sport," said Tracy, nervously. Gloria and Henry came running in.

"How are you, Jon, love? Feeling better?"

"Yes, I think so. Wasn't that fantastic?"

Gloria and Henry looked at each other and back at him again.

"Incredible. It's all over the news! Most dramatic, dear. Nobody can really believe it. Except *her* of course. She seems to have no problems accepting anything. Quite a forceful lady, all in all."

"Isn't she beautiful?" said Jonathan, nervously.

"Yes, she's certainly beautiful," said Henry and Gloria in unison.

"She just borrowed $500 off Henry," mentioned Gloria.

"Yes, she needs some clothes and things I think," answered Jonathan. He was beginning to tingle. "You'd better help me to the hotel."

On the way out they passed the wheelchair, discarded.

"We won't be needing that anymore," said Henry, with artificial humour.

The crowd had dispersed outside the theatre. Most of them had apparently followed the mannequin, hoping for autographs and photos.

"She told me to organise some postcard handout pictures for her," said Tracy. "I've got a feeling she'll need 'em."

An assistant floor manager rushed ahead of them.

"Good night," he said with a wave.

Abe Pursen had already left, with other pressing business to attend to. He'd asked Henry to relay his congratulations to Jonathan with the specific message that the final collapse had been a magnificent touch, quite unexpected and an absolute bonus.

"The camera zoomed in on you as you lay at her feet, Jon," Tracy said, "and then did one of those split screen jobs on her face as well, and the orchestra soared off into a rousing version of 'America the Beautiful' and the audience rose to its feet applauding louder than you've ever heard and whistling and trumpeting and Abe said 'goodnight' very low and deep and respectful. It was tremendous."

Jonathan was very quiet.

They got back to the Waldorf and went to their respective rooms. Jonathan locked his door and lay on the bed. He felt empty, betrayed, void of the ability to cry or rage. He had achieved his goal, as the pile of congratulatory cards and messages verified, but it meant nothing. It was a hollow victory. The mannequin had shed every quality that had attracted him to her.

Was the fault his own, he wondered? Had he only imagined the graceful dignity she had possessed? Or had he himself destroyed it, in his relentless pursuit of the impossible? For that was as he now saw it. The rest of the world had witnessed the miracle, the breathing of life into an inanimate shell, but he realised that the event proved finally that his ambitions had been lunatic and worthless.

The bottomless misery was somehow cleansing. He closed his eyes and went into a deep, comatose, dreamless sleep. No more circuses. No more ambition.

He woke early and began to pack his bags. There was a pounding of fists on his door. He opened it and Henry and Gloria fell in, clutching copies of a newspaper in vivid and gaudy colours.

"Christ, that little bastard's really done it this time," panted Henry. "Look!"

Although slightly eclipsed by the dramatic events of the TV show which nobody had anticipated, Pirraner's epic was stunning. He had, for the first and only time in his life, written a masterpiece. Corruption was hinted at without being specific, names were repeated in unfortunate contexts, depravity was described without guaranteed connections, but any reader would assume that the quest had been one long trail of perversion and dishonesty from start to finish. At least half a dozen careers were ruined, a number of family lives terminated, some suicides provoked and a great deal of official inquiries started.

Jonathan continued his packing.

"It's awful, love. Look at the things he's said about you! How can he get away with these lies? You must sue him, love."

Henry realised Jonathan was not particularly concerned.

"There's worse news, I'm afraid," Henry said. "You know I've been trying to speak to you for ages about the company, but you wouldn't listen. Well, matters haven't gone too well," he blustered, vaguely. "You know I only just started all this executive trip, dear, when you took me on. I like to think I did a good job all considered. But I didn't know, then, how to delegate responsibilities and pick new people to run the business. And I fear my own involvement with the publishing area meant I rather deserted your interests, Jonathan. Junior employees suggested investing in a lot of commodities and shares and they've not been doing too well."

He paused. Jonathan was folding a light blue sweater and tucking it into the corner of his Revelation suitcase.

"They've not been doing too well at all," he repeated. "In fact, the corporation is heavily in debt. I've sold off a lot of stock. I *did* keep asking you, dear," he justified to himself, "and I'm afraid there's precious little left. In fact, this newspaper story will squash any credibility Farting International ever had. Jonathan," he said, realising he was going to have to put it bluntly to get through at all, "you haven't got any money, darling."

Jonathan made a ball out of a couple of socks and squashed them into a departing shoe.

"Don't blame yourself, Henry," he said. "The fault was entirely mine. I must thank you for your loyalty – both of you. I shall now return to Farting Castle and live the life of a hermit in contemplation and peace."

"Er, there's even a problem with that, sweetie," said Henry. "I've had to sell the castle to pay some of the estate debts. Don't worry," he added, hastily, "I've managed to keep it in the family. I've bought it myself, and, of course, you're welcome to stay there whenever you like."

"So is there nothing left?" asked Jonathan, more out of interest than any great concern.

"Well, yes, there is one asset which belongs to you

173

personally and the creditors could not touch. The laywers finally sorted out that trust last week and the stables are definitely yours, if you want them."

Jonathan flinched.

"Naturally you can sell them if you like. They're not worth as much as they were, but, with grounds and all that, they should fetch a few thousand pounds. . .honey."

The "honey" was tentative and nervous. Henry obviously felt very badly that he'd let his dear friend down in so many ways.

Jonathan went over and put his arms around them both. "Don't concern yourselves. I hope we shall always be fond and close acquaintances. The stables will do fine for me. I think I deserve them."

There were tears in Gloria's eyes and even Henry looked touched.

"Give my regards to Tracy," said Jonathan, giving them each a squeeze and carrying his case out into the hallway.

"Let me get you a porter," cried Henry.

"No, that's all right," said Jonathan, "I'll do it myself."

Autumn in Berkshire is very lovely indeed. The leaves turn colours painters cannot capture. The sun does a great deal of dappling and dancing with shadows. In the evening, just before nightfall, the light is so mellow that it doesn't seem to come from the sun anymore, but from the horizon and the sky and the plants of the earth.

Jonathan never did get to like horses, but they put up with each other. Henry and Gloria got married almost immediately, as Gloria discovered she was pregnant, but Jonathan didn't see much of his neighbours except on feast days and celebrations. He was, however, asked to be godfather to their first child, a compliment which he quietly declined. Henry's em-

174

pire grew and grew. He was knighted and eventually made a lord.

· Andy Pirraner wrote a bestselling book based on the events he had so closely witnessed. In order to accomplish maximum public appeal, the viciousness was watered down and the uplifting climax exaggerated. Andy didn't really mind this. He was exceedingly rich and lived in great comfort, writing the occasional op-ed piece for the *New York Times*. Strangely, he was never so content as he had been in those days and nights spent labouring at a desk in the YMCA. He liked Manhattan, though. Its pace suited his style. And he voraciously commented in print about the disgraceful and overwhelming increase of violent crime in his neighbourhood.

David Kraft spent a long time trying to persuade Abe Pursen to run for President, and, when he failed, decided to do so himself. He achieved the office with the greatest of ease. He ruled long and fair over the citizens of the United States, keeping tight control of the organs of publicity and making sure that every decision was made only after lengthy consultation with Abe Pursen, a wise and decent counsellor.

Tracy went to live in Adelaide and married a sheep farmer. It was some years before she admitted to him she'd been born in Finchley and had never been further west than New York City before deciding on her emigration. Veronica Tweed survived the allegations over her participation in the Farting affair only to fall from grace when a serious flaw was discovered in her election expense returns. She was represented in court by Sir Dimly Vial, QC and, although cleared of all charges, she retired to local politics and married a stockbroker. Sir Dimly himself went on to be Master of the Rolls and a most important judge indeed, quite befitting his knowledge of, and love for, the law and the legal profession.

Dr Peter Smooth was visited in prison on a regular basis by his brother. Whilst there he was extremely popular with the other convicts and provided analysis free of charge. On release he continued his practise and built up a formidable array of important clients. His brother sadly succumbed to cancer of the lung and passed away at an early age.

Sir Newton Bean and Mr Gross remained where they were, ageless and timeless, the one a respected and ancient professor of learning, never changing, and the other a capable and efficient shop manager, keeping Selfishes the fine store it has always been.

The mannequin flew to Hollywood, changed her name to Manny Quinn and won her own TV chat show, which became stratospherically popular and survives at the top of the ratings, on ABS, to this very day. Her poise and natural ability are the pride of America; her dignity and style, the apogee of culture; her skill in listening and questioning, the ultimate in art. Abe Pursen is very proud of her, but only talks to her agent.